WONDROUS CHRISTMAS STORIES

Edited by Anne Finnis

Scholastic Children's Books
Commonwealth House
1–19 New Oxford Street,
London WC1A 1NU
a division of Scholastic Ltd
London ~ New York ~ Toronto ~ Sydney ~ Auckland

First published in the UK by Scholastic Ltd, 1997

This anthology copyright © Scholastic Ltd, 1997

ISBN 0 590 54268 0

Typeset by TW Typesetting, Midsomer Norton, Somerset
Printed by Clays Ltd, St Ives plc

Acknowledgements

All the stories are original and appear for the first time in this volume.

The following are the copyright owners of the stories:

Just Like an Angel copyright © 1997 Gillian Cross

A Funny Sort of Christmas copyright © 1997 Ann Ruffell

The Worst Christmas Ever copyright © 1997 Malorie Blackman

Mr Mackintosh copyright © 1997 Aileen Paterson

Not Just For Christmas... copyright © 1997 Rob Childs

Kookaburra Christmas copyright © 1997 Herbie Brennan

The Christmas Squirrel copyright © 1997 Philippa Gregory

Billy's Christmas Surprises copyright © 1997 Malcolm Yorke

The Real Christmas Play copyright © 1997 Geraldine Kaye

The Umbrella Tree Fairy copyright © 1997 Jean Ure

Snowstorm copyright © 1997 Adèle Geras

The Greatest Gift of All copyright © 1997 Jenny Bent

Sparrow's Special Christmas copyright © 1997 Susan Gates

Dear Santa copyright © 1997 Tessa Krailing

Contents

Just Like an Angel

Gillian Cross

Gabriel was the youngest in the family, and he wasn't like his brothers. Michael, Richard and Edward were long-legged and cheerful, with blond hair and blue eyes, but Gabriel was small and shy. The others teased him about everything.

Especially angels.

It started when he was four. They were on their way to stay with Grandmother, for the Christmas carol service. As they drove into her village, Gabriel looked out of the car window and saw big, white shapes circling in the sky. They were moving slowly, with the winter sunlight glancing off their wings.

They weren't aeroplanes. Gabriel knew that aeroplanes moved faster, and made a noise. He lifted his hand and pointed.

"Look! Angels!"

Michael and Richard and Edward fell about laughing.

"Hey, Mum! Gabe thinks those are *angels*!"

"Leave him alone," Mrs Jennings said. "They're gliders, Gabriel. Like aeroplanes without engines. They ride on the air currents."

Her voice was kind, but she was laughing too. She couldn't help it. As they drove up the main street of the village, she stopped at the petrol pumps, and told Mr King the garage man, speaking slowly and clearly, so that he could see what she was saying.

"Gabriel thought the gliders were angels."

Gabriel shrank back into the car, waiting for Mr King to laugh. But he didn't. He stroked his long beard, thoughtfully, and smiled into the car.

"Funny you should say that. I often think the same thing, when I'm up in my glider. *Just like being an angel…*"

Suddenly, Gabriel didn't feel stupid any more. He sat up straight, and smiled back at Mr King. And his brothers leaned out of the car windows, calling out in loud, clear voices.

"Have you really got a glider?"

"Will you take us up in it?"

"Please!"

There was no more teasing that day. But Michael

and Richard and Edward didn't forget. All the year, they roared with laughter if anyone mentioned angels. And when they were on the way to Grandmother's again, next Christmas, Michael pointed up at the sky.

"Hey, Gabe! After the carol service – when I've sung the solo – we might go up in Mr King's glider."

"*Really?*" Gabriel's eyes glittered, and he bounced up and down in his seat. "Me too?"

"Why don't you ask?" Michael said solemnly. "Look, we're just going past the garage."

Gabriel was so excited that he stuck his head out of the window. "Mr King! Can *I* go in your glider?"

"What's that?" Mr King came forward, out of his little glass cabin. "Say it again, lad."

But Michael didn't give him a chance. He stuck his head out too. "Gabriel wants a ride in your glider. He thinks he'll turn into an angel."

Mr King didn't laugh, but Gabriel realized that it was just a tease. He went pink and pulled his head back into the car.

The next day, Michael sang the solo at the carol service, and all the old ladies muttered about what an angel he was. Gabriel shrank down into the pew. It felt just as if they were laughing at him.

That was Michael's last year as an angel. In June, his voice broke, and he couldn't do anything except growl and croak. When Christmas came, it was Richard who sang the solo. And two years after that, Edward had to take over.

It was a tradition in Grandmother's village. The first verse of the first carol had always been sung as a solo, by a child.

> *O come, all ye faithful,*
> *Joyful and triumphant,*
> *O come ye, O come ye*
> *To Bethlehem…*

But there were no children in the choir any more – hardly any children in the village, in fact. So, every year, one of Gabriel's brothers sang instead, with his fair hair gleaming and his blue eyes bright. And all the old men in the congregation smiled, and the old women dabbed at their eyes.

And Gabriel sat there wondering how Michael (or Richard or Edward) could be so brave. Singing in front of all those people.

Then, when Gabriel was eight, Edward's voice

broke. One day, just before Christmas, he came down to breakfast and started singing, and everyone burst out laughing.

Gabriel laughed too – but not for long. Because Edward grinned at him.

"Looks like you'll be singing the solo this Christmas."

"*Me?*" It came out in a strangled squeak.

"You!" Michael and Richard and Edward yelled. And they laughed even more. They thought he was fussing about nothing.

"It's easy," Michael said. "You just need a bit of practice."

They stood Gabriel on a chair and Richard started humming, pretending to be the organ. "Come on, now. Sing. *O come all ye faithful...*"

Gabriel tried. But the more he tried, the less noise he could make. When he looked round at the three of them, all staring, he felt as if he were choking to death. The only sound that would come out of his mouth was a strangled squeak.

"*O cme all ye fthfl...*"

The others burst out laughing and he jumped off the chair and ran upstairs. And after that, when anyone suggested practising, he looked away and mumbled that he'd done enough practising.

"Dne nff pracsing."

Everyone believed him. And they were sure he would be all right. Why shouldn't he be? Singing was easy. Nobody knew how scared he was.

The nearer they got to Christmas, the worse it grew. When they were actually in the car, on the way to Grandmother's, he was so scared that he thought he was going to faint. He couldn't smile, even though his brothers tried all the old jokes.

"Look, Gabe. Angels up in the sky!"

"Mr King's going to give us a ride in one of those gliders."

"After you've sung your solo."

Gabriel turned away and stared out of the window. He knew he was running out of time. When they arrived at Grandmother's, he had to go straight to bed. And the next day it was the carol service.

The moment he opened his eyes, he thought, *I've got to practise. Before it's too late.* Maybe he would be all right if he found a place where no one could hear him.

He walked down to the far end of the garden and hid behind a rhododendron bush. But the moment he opened his mouth, he began to worry that someone would come. And he made the same strangled sounds as before. *O cme all ye fthful…*

He tried locking himself in the bathroom and turning on all the taps. But was the noise really loud enough to drown out his voice? Before he could make up his mind, Grandmother banged on the door, to ask him why he was wasting all that water.

He tried putting his head under the bedclothes, with all the pillows heaped on top. But that just made him suffocate, so that he gasped and panted. *O-ho c-h-me all ye f-h-thf-h-l…*

And then it was lunchtime. And he'd just picked up his knife and fork when Grandmother said, "All ready for the rehearsal then, Gabriel?"

"Rehearsal?" Gabriel stared.

Michael grinned. "Gabriel doesn't need a rehearsal."

"Nonsense!" Grandmother said briskly. "You all went to the rehearsal. That's why you sang so well. Gabriel must rehearse too. I'll take him down to church as soon as we've washed up."

Gabriel had forgotten about the rehearsal. He'd hardly noticed last year, when Edward slipped off to church in the afternoon. But he remembered now, and he knew he couldn't do it.

He couldn't walk into the church with Grand-mother, and stand in front of all those men and women in the choir and sing *O cme all ye fthfl...* He couldn't.

He would have to run away.

He didn't manage to eat much lunch, but every-one just smiled and said he was excited. Then they all went off to the kitchen to wash up in Double Quick Time. Grandmother liked everything done in Double Quick Time. Gabriel waited until they were laughing and talking and teasing each other. Then he opened the front door and slipped out.

There were only two ways to go – left and right. The road to the left went up to the church, so he turned the other way, automatically. He went downhill, towards the garage, running as fast as he could, to get out of sight before anyone saw him.

He ran too fast. As he passed the garage, he caught his foot on a loose stone and went tumbling over, scraping his knees along the ground and banging his head on the Tarmac.

For a moment he just lay there, thinking that things were as bad as they could possibly be. Then he remembered that they would be even worse if anyone caught him, because he'd have to go to the rehearsal. He groaned and started dragging himself up.

But he was too late. Mr King had seen him fall over. He came out of the little glass office behind the petrol pumps and inspected Gabriel's knees.

"Nasty fall," he said calmly. "Come in and have a barley sugar."

For a moment, Gabriel thought of running away. Then he realized that Mr King might run after him. He followed him into the glass cabin, limping a bit.

Mr King unhooked a bag of barley sugars from the display, opened it and gave one to Gabriel. Then he said, "What are you doing down here this afternoon? I thought you'd be up at the church. Rehearsing."

That was the last straw. Before he could stop himself, Gabriel burst into tears.

Mr King pulled a handkerchief out of his pocket and unfolded it. He watched Gabriel wipe his eyes and then said, "What's up?"

"Gt t sng n the crl svice," mumbled Gabriel, with his face in his hands. "Nd m scared—"

"No use talking like that," Mr King said. "You know I can't hear. Take your hands away from your mouth and let me lip-read."

Gabriel had forgotten Mr King was deaf. Dropping his hands, he made himself speak clearly. He was concentrating so hard on making the shapes of the words with his lips, that he didn't worry about what he was saying.

"I've got to sing the solo at the carol service. And I'm scared."

Mr King nodded. "Not surprised. There's only one way to get over that. Practice."

Gabriel hung his head. "Bt—" Then he remembered about Mr King's deafness, and he started again. "But if I practise, the others laugh at me."

"So you can't sing? In case they laugh?"

Gabriel nodded.

Mr King gave him another barely sugar and walked up and down for a bit. Then he stopped and looked at Gabriel.

"Want to come up in a glider?"

"Me?" Gabriel was so amazed that he didn't mumble at all. Mr King had never offered any of the others a flight. Even though they'd begged him, for years and years. "Just me?"

"Just you," Mr King said. "Come on."

They walked out of the cabin and he locked it behind them. Then he turned the big sign at the front of the forecourt, so that it said CLOSED instead of OPEN.

"We've just got time before it's too dark. If we hurry."

They climbed into his Land Rover and it started with a judder and bounced down the hill towards Mr King's house. When they got there, Mr King put on the brake, very noisily, and said something.

Gabriel couldn't hear at first, because of the engine. Then he remembered about lip-reading and he saw what Mr King was saying. *Wait there while I fetch my brothers.*

There were two brothers. They both had beards, but one was fat and one was thin. They smiled as they climbed into the back of the Land Rover. With a crash of gears, Mr King drove out of the village and up to the glider field.

Gabriel had been to the field dozens of times. Whenever they came to the village, his brothers walked up there and stared longingly at the hangar where Mr King kept his red and white glider. If he was there, Mr King would smile and wave to them, but he never asked them into the field.

This time, he drove straight in and round the track at the edge of the field.

"Stay in the Land Rover," he said to Gabriel.

Gabriel knew what was going to happen, because he'd seen it before. He watched Mr King's brothers open the hangar and wheel out the glider. He watched Mr King prepare the winch, and unwind the long cable that would pull the glider into the air.

The brothers settled the glider at the far end of the field and left it there, with the sun gleaming on its red and white paint. Then they came back up to the hangar. The fat brother found a helmet.

"Scared?" he said, as he adjusted the straps round Gabriel's chin.

"No." Gabriel didn't see how anyone could be scared about going up in a glider. How could you be afraid of something wonderful?

Climbing into the cockpit, he settled himself in the front seat, with Mr King behind him. His heart was thudding against his ribs, but he knew he wasn't scared. He was excited.

The thin brother held on to the glider's wing and the fat one went down the field, to start the winch.

Suddenly, the glider was racing forward, pulled by the cable. The thin brother ran along beside, holding it level.

"Here we go!" said Mr King.

And the glider took off.

It went up like a bird. Like an arrow shot from a bow. Rising into the air like something speeding up a steep, steep hill. Gabriel felt himself being pushed against the back of his seat. Up and up and up…

And then they stopped climbing.

"Look over the side," Mr King's voice said, from behind.

Gabriel turned his head and saw the winch cable falling away as the glider levelled out. The cable had done its work and pulled them up, just as the string pulls a kite. Now they were in the sky, floating free. Riding the currents of the air.

It was very quiet. The only sounds Gabriel could hear were the creak of the wooden wings and the hiss of air round his head. He was sitting high in the sky, with nothing to shut him in.

Far below, he could see the village. The church where the choir was singing. The cars racing round the bypass. A train in the distance. They were all too far away to hear.

For a few minutes, the glider circled slowly, and Gabriel stared round. He was amazed how clearly he could see everything, even though it was such a long way down. It was like looking at the whole world.

"Beautiful, isn't it?" Mr King said.

Gabriel nodded. There was no way of saying how beautiful it was.

Mr King gave a small, soft chuckle. "Always makes me want to sing."

"*Do* you sing?" Gabriel said. "Up here on your own?"

There was another chuckle. "No use talking. I can't lip-read from here. Can't hear a thing you're saying."

For a second, Gabriel felt stupid.

And then he understood what Mr King was telling him. They were up there on their own, just the two of them. And Mr King was deaf. *So no one could possibly hear any singing. No one in the whole world!*

But – wasn't it ridiculous? Singing in a glider?

Gabriel looked over the side, at the grey church spire, and the glittering line of the brook, and the big hills stretching away into the distance. The lovely, sunlit world. No, singing wasn't ridiculous. It was the only sensible thing to do.

He opened his mouth.

O come all ye faithful,
Joyful and triumphant...

It felt wonderful. Like yelling hurrah. Like blowing a fanfare on a trumpet.

Like being an angel.

The white wings of the glider gleamed in the winter sunshine. There was a small green car driving round the bypass. Maybe there was a little boy inside. Looking up at the glider and thinking it was an angel. Gabriel took a deep breath and sang as loudly and sweetly as he could.

O come let us adore him,
O come let us adore him,
O come let us adore him,
Christ the Lord!

He was still singing as the glider circled lower over the field. He didn't even realize they were landing, until they bumped lightly on to the grass, and Mr King's brothers came running forward to help him out of his seat.

"That was a nice bit of singing," said the thin brother.

"Look forward to hearing you in church," said the fat brother.

Gabriel went pink and hung his head. "Bt tht's diffrnt."

Mr King tapped his shoulder. "What did you say?"

Gabriel felt silly, but he turned round and spoke clearly. "I said that's different. Singing in church."

"Don't see why," Mr King said. "Shut your eyes, and you can be anywhere you like."

The brothers both nodded, and Gabriel frowned. What did they mean?

"Time to go home," Mr King said. "I'll take you up. These two will put the glider away. Hop in the Land Rover, lad."

As Gabriel climbed in, he suddenly wondered what he was going to say when he got back to Grandmother's house. She would be furious with him. How could he explain why he'd run away?

He didn't have to explain anything. When they

reached the house, Mr King went in on his own, leaving Gabriel to wait in the Land Rover. When he came out again, Grandmother was with him. She was smiling.

"You've missed the rehearsal, but it sounds as though you don't need one. Mr King tells me you're a wonderful singer."

"But—" *But Mr King can't hear...*

Grandmother didn't give Gabriel time to say it. She caught hold of his arm. "Hurry up, or we'll be late for the service."

Michael came bounding out of the house in his best clothes. "Gabriel can't go to church like that. He's wearing jeans."

"Don't be silly," Grandmother said. "And anyway, no one will see when he's got the choir robes on. Come along, Gabriel."

She hustled him down the path, with the rest of the family scurrying behind. Michael ran to catch up, whispering in Gabriel's ear.

"Where have you been?"

"In a glider," Gabriel said.

"Oh, ha ha!" Michael pulled a face. "Stop teasing."

Teasing? "Mr King took me up."

Richard jogged up. "Don't be silly. The garage is open on Friday afternoons. Mr King must have been there."

Gabriel couldn't answer, because they'd reached the church, and Grandmother was chivvying him round to the vestry. She buttoned him into a long blue cassock and slipped a white surplice over his head. Then she nodded approvingly.

"You look very nice. Even better than your brothers."

Gabriel didn't care how he looked. As she pushed him into line with the rest of the choir, he was shaking. And when they walked into church, he nearly fainted. All the front pews were full. People were going to *hear* him. He couldn't sing. He *couldn't*.

The organist began the introduction to the first carol. Gabriel felt his throat go dry. He knew he wouldn't be able to make any sound except a squeak. He knew it. But there was no escape.

He opened his mouth.

And then, at the last moment, he saw Mr King, sitting at the back of the church, looking at him. Slowly and deliberately, Mr King closed his eyes. *Shut your eyes, and you can be anywhere you like.*

All at once, Gabriel understood. He closed his own eyes – and he wasn't looking at rows of people any more. He was in the glider, circling like an angel. The sunshine was glittering on the snow-white wings, and the beautiful world was spread out below.

He started to sing, as sweetly as he could.

O come all ye faithful…

He didn't open his eyes until the whole carol was over. When he did, he saw his brothers, sitting in the front pew, staring at him. Wondering whether it could be possibly true about the glider. He almost burst out laughing.

But he didn't laugh. He stared straight ahead, looking solemn and good, and he heard the old ladies whispering to each other.

"Just like an angel…"

I'll do it even better next year, he thought. And he started smiling. He had years and years left before his voice broke. Years and years of being a Christmas angel.

A Funny Sort of Christmas

Ann Ruffell

It had been a funny sort of Christmas. There was no snow. It wasn't even cold. Ruth's parents had put the log fire on because it wouldn't have seemed like Christmas without it, but as the day wore on people moved further and further back from it.

Most of Christmas had been the same as usual. There were visits from aunts and uncles and two grannies. Everyone played board games, even her brother Ben. An uncle she had never seen telephoned from Australia.

This happened every year.

And every year before Christmas Mum and Dad told Ruth to write a letter to Santa and send it up the chimney. Every year she wrote her letter. It seemed to go by special chimney post direct to the North Pole, because every year, by magic, the thing she wanted appeared under the Christmas tree.

But this year it didn't.

Ruth had to be fair about this. It was probably just too expensive for even Father Christmas to buy. And definitely it was too expensive for her parents to buy.

But when her friend Chrissie rang up halfway through Christmas morning to say she'd been given a clarinet, Ruth did feel that *someone* could have managed a xylophone.

She would gladly have traded *all* the chocolates and games and soft toys and bubble bath for a xylophone. If all her relations had clubbed together, perhaps they could have afforded one.

Ruth and Chrissie wanted to have music lessons at school. Ben and Hannah, her older brother and sister, were already in the school orchestra. It all sounded such a lot of fun that Ruth wanted to be in it as soon as she went to senior school.

But you can't join an orchestra if you don't play anything.

You could borrow violins and clarinets and trumpets from school and learn on them. Chrissie had been given a school clarinet to bring home so that she could practise.

But the school didn't own a xylophone, and you can't practise a xylophone if you haven't got one.

What was worse, now she would have to wait until she got into the senior school even to have lessons.

But it wasn't fair to sulk. There simply wasn't enough money for things like a xylophone. Ruth thought she would try to work herself up to playing the violin.

Christmas Day turned into evening. Ben and Hannah had gone out to a party. Mum was tired out with cooking and Dad was tired out with whisky. They said they thought of going to bed.

"Can I stay up and watch the film?" asked Ruth.

Mum stared through the TV pages. There didn't seem to be anything unsuitable, and after all, it was Christmas.

"And I'll wash up. Really, I'd like to."

"You don't have to bother," yawned Mum, "but I wouldn't mind if you did."

After they had gone to bed, Ruth listened for a while to the creakings and mutterings from the apartment upstairs, getting to know them so that she knew what the strange night noises were. From her own bedroom, at night, she could only hear the traffic outside, and she had never been up, alone, so late before. Then she slipped a tape into the cassette player in the kitchen and turned the volume down.

She ran a basin full of soapy water into the sink, and put the dishes in it to soak. The hollow, stone-like xylophone tune of *Danse Macabre* from the cassette player blended pleasantly with the chime of dirty dishes. Then she took the plateful of turkey bones downstairs to the big dustbin in the basement.

Just as she got to the bottom of the stairs the light bulb flashed and went out. There was just enough light from upstairs to see where the door to the bin was. It was a dark, windowless, smelly place.

The bin's sides were maggot white in the light struggling down from upstairs. The lid was thick black, blacker than the darkness all around. It looked like a deep hole going right down to the bottom of the world.

But it isn't, Ruth told herself firmly. It's just a dustbin. And, feeling very grown up and sensible, she lifted the lid. She had to tug at it quite hard. She was all ready to tip the plate of bones, clamp the lid down, and run back upstairs before her courage ran out.

But a strange, whitish, greenish glow came from

inside. Goosepimples grew up on her skin and froze her to the spot. From down inside the dustbin's black hole something rose up, clattering as it came. A twig-like hand stretched out for the plate. It scooped up the turkey bones and arranged some of them into a smile.

"Thanks," said the smile. "Forgive the gear but you can't get human teeth too often these days."

The little bones of a wrist anchored themselves on to the side of the dustbin. Bony fingers waggled about for a hand-hold. Then a whole rope of bones heaved themselves out, shook themselves and smiled with a slightly different arrangement of ivories.

It was a skeleton.

It was made of bones from the turkey as well as from an assorted collection of those from lamb chops, chicken wings and pork knuckles. It was odd, but somehow not – really – frightening.

"So you weren't satisfied, eh?"

Ruth found that even though her tongue was dry, it still worked.

"I – don't know what you mean—"

"Sure you do. No xylo. Shame, but we had to think of your neighbours, you know. Get complaints, about drums and hi-fi and so on. Not always our fault. But when there's genuine hardship, we like to explain."

"Who – who are you?" stammered Ruth.

"Santa's little helper, of course," said the skeleton. "What did you think I was?"

"But I thought…"

"I suppose you're worried about these," said the skeleton, pointing at its teeth which were not molars now but pieces of rabbit rib. "Not perfect, but the best I could do under the circumstances. The trouble with people going vegetarian is that it's not easy to build up a shape to talk to our customers. Your family now – they're really good carnivores. Nice to make your acquaintance."

"How – how do you do?" said Ruth. Surely it didn't mean her to shake the bony hand? She tried to explain again. "But I thought…"

"You thought He had an army of dwarfs? And that He drives about on Christmas night with a sleigh and a herd of reindeer? Rudolph the Red-Nosed thingummy and all that?"

"Well – yes," said Ruth.

"I can never get Him to tell people the truth," sighed the skeleton. "The thing is…" He stopped.

"People like the sleigh and the reindeer, but the fact is we're spirits. Ghosts, if you like. And we have to use whatever you've left lying about to make ourselves into something that won't frighten you."

Ruth thought a skeleton was quite frightening enough, thank you. But she was too polite to say so. The skeleton was obviously trying very hard.

"Do you fancy a game now I'm here?" it went on. "You look as if you could use some company. How about hide and creak, Tibial Pursuit, something of that sort?"

"I wanted to be alone," said Ruth. This was a mistake. You are only alone with other people who have nothing to say to you. It did seem perfectly friendly, but she did not want to be alone with a skeleton.

"Nonsense," said the collection of bones. "It's Christmas, and you've got a reasonable complaint. It's the least I can do to cheer you up. Do you prefer knucklebones or hangman?"

"I'm cold," said Ruth, who was shivering right down her own backbone. "I'm going back upstairs to the fire."

Perhaps if she went up to the light the ghostly apparition might disappear back into the shadows.

However, the skeleton appeared to enjoy the thought of warmth. It followed her, chattering hollowly, all the way back upstairs. Finally it settled down in front of the fire with a clacking like a fast game of fivestones.

"Can we have some music?" it asked. "Not organs or choirs. I'm sick of them. You get nothing else at funerals."

"What sort of thing would you like?" asked Ruth, moving towards the CD player. "Something cheerful?"

"Something to dance to," said the skeleton. "Let me have a look."

"Oh, do be careful!" cried Ruth anxiously as the skeleton poked its bony fingers into Dad's carefully arranged collection of CDs. She was far more afraid of Dad's anger than of a mere skeleton. "Don't scratch anything."

"Can't. No nails," said the skeleton. "Ah, this one will do." It put a disc into the machine, and the air was filled with the hollow xylophone tones of *Fossils* from Saint Saens' *Carnival of the Animals*.

"Lovely, isn't it?" it said, beginning to jerk and gyrate round the room. It danced tirelessly to the end of the music, then Ruth hurried to turn off the stereo before the assortment of relics should try to do so itself and ruin something.

But the skeleton had already seen something else which interested it. The flat was big, with high ceilings and built-in cupboards in every room. It wrenched at the knob of one of these. It wasn't exactly a cupboard but a windowless space as big as a small room between the dining-room and the sitting-room. Mum kept her computer there and Dad used the place as a dark room where he developed his own films. Ruth didn't see the skeleton turn it on, but suddenly there was a red glow from the ruby bulb.

"Do you think we ought…" she began, but the skeleton turned to her with a great champing of enjoyment from its already grinning jaws.

"Skeletons in the cupboard," it tittered. "Have a look."

The keys of the computer played a fanfare of complex rhythms. On the screen in green light, a whole chorus line of skeletons oozed out of the margin to dance from right to left before disappearing back into the machine.

"What disk is that on?" marvelled Ruth.

"Disk?" said the skeleton. "I don't need a disk.

Only a few slipped into the backbone!" It laughed like a heap of recycled cans at his own joke.

"Then how…?"

But the skeleton was bored with the computer. It peered with empty eye sockets at the strip of developed black and white film hanging from a nail.

"Shall I?" it asked. "Oh, why not!"

It wasn't until Dad printed the pictures a week later that Ruth understood what it had meant. You had to look very closely before you saw the skulls, one cunningly concealed in each picture like those puzzles in magazines.

"What can we do now?" it said. "Is there any more music?"

"In the kitchen," said Ruth, anxious to get it away in case it wiped either the pictures from the film or something terribly important from the computer. "I was washing up."

"Washing up? I've never washed up in my death! Is it fun?"

"Well, not really…"

"Can I do some? Only you mustn't blame me if anything gets broken. I haven't had as much practice as you. Still, hard work breaks no bones!"

Ruth wound the tape back and switched on

Danse Macabre for it.

"You like the old xylo then?" said the skeleton conversationally, picking up a cup from the draining board. "Your favourite thing?"

"Yes," said Ruth shortly. She didn't want to talk about it. She was getting over it nicely.

"Must say I quite agree with you, great stuff," it said, jerking about as it dried. The cup slipped from its uncoordinated metacarpals and fell on to the floor.

"Only the handle," said the skeleton, but its grinning jaw dropped a little.

"It's Dad's favourite cup," said Ruth. It mattered a little, but not as much as if they had damaged any records.

"I could mend it, if you boil up my fish bones for glue."

"I can't boil *you* up to make glue!" said Ruth.

"Don't see why not," said the skeleton. "Can you think of anything better?"

"There's a tube on top of the fridge," said Ruth.

The skeleton sniffed a little. "That stuff's only chemical rubbish," it sneered. "Still, if that's what you want..."

It put a stool on top of a chair to reach. It wavered,

wobbled, made a grab at the tube of glue, then crashed to the ground in a charnel heap of bones.

"Not to worry," said the lower jaw from the side of the cooker. "Give me half a minute. I'll soon pull myself together."

Ruth clucked round its components like a motherly hen. "Are you sure you're all right? Can I help? Here's a leg bone – oh, no, it isn't, it's…"

But the skeleton was happily picking up pieces of itself and sticking them into the right places.

"You need a good course in basic anatomy, that's what you need," it said scathingly. "Now give me that cup and I'll stick the handle on while you finish the washing up. I told you it wasn't my thing." It hummed a few bars from *Danse Macabre* as it worked. "There you are. Good as new."

"Upside down," said Ruth unkindly.

"Don't be finicky," said the skeleton. "Still, I suppose you'd know." It pulled the handle off and turned it round the right way. "Is that better?"

"Lovely," said Ruth. "Now I've got to shake the tablecloth and we've finished."

"Let me do that," begged the skeleton. "I love waving white cloths about."

It rattled into the dining-room and hauled the

cloth, salt and pepper and a small vase of flowers from the table. The salt and pepper pots rolled on to the floor, and the flowers lay in a pool of water which was rapidly soaked up by the carpet. The skeleton stumbled back into the kitchen.

"I'm sorry, but I don't seem able to get out of this tablecloth," it said in a muffled voice. "Your glue is very powerful."

Just then there was a knock at the door.

"Oh, dear," said Ruth, "there are Ben and Hannah back from their party. It looks as if they've forgotten their key again."

"They need a skeleton key!" sniggered the skeleton, and wafted towards the front door.

"No!" cried Ruth, following it. "Perhaps I'd better…"

"Don't be silly, I can reach quite well," said the stifled voice beneath the tablecloth. "I'll do it." And before Ruth could stop it, the skeleton had unlocked the front door and swung it open.

"You took your ti – *crikey*!" said Hannah.

"Come on, Ruth, we know it's you," said Ben, and poked the cloth.

An owl hooted, twice, and the tablecloth fell to the ground with a tattoo of hollow noise.

"Honestly, Ruth, if you think you can frighten us…" said Ben.

"I thought you were underneath it," said Hannah, seeing Ruth come up from behind. "How did you do it? Broom handle?" She lifted the cloth.

Underneath was a xylophone. It was very small, but perfect in every detail. And it was made out of the bones of pork knuckle, turkey and chicken, with rabbit rib for the very highest notes.

"Did you do it while we were out? It's really good."

Ben seized a stray shin bone and struck it lightly. It gave out a sweet, high, hollow sound, perfectly in tune.

It was the most beautiful thing she had ever seen. A present from Father Christmas.

Ben and Hannah had shut the door and were exclaiming over it. She would let them try it out, but later. Just now, it was all hers.

"Wait a bit, the glue's not quite dry," said Ruth. "The cloth got stuck on it." She picked up the xylophone and took it in to the warm sitting-room.

She didn't think she'd tell them about the skeleton. They'd never believe her, and there wasn't any need.

It really had been a very funny Christmas.

The Worst Christmas Ever

Malorie Blackman

I'm only writing this because Mr Cooling, my teacher, says I have to. I don't particularly want to write about my Christmas. It was the worst Christmas ever. I know everyone in my class thinks I'm lucky because I always get everything I want – but that all changed this Christmas. I really don't want to talk about this. It still upsets me to think about it – and I think about it a lot. But as I don't seem to have much choice – here goes.

Two or three weeks before Christmas, Mum and Dad sat me down in my own special armchair. They sat opposite me on the sofa. I smiled at them. I knew what was going to come next, or at least, I thought I did.

"You're going to ask me what I want for Christmas, aren't you?" I said, excited. "I've already made my Christmas list. I want the new computer game, the one called…"

"Kathini, we're not here to talk about Christmas presents," Dad interrupted.

That was when I noticed their faces. Mum and Dad looked so sad and sombre.

"What's the matter?" I asked.

"It's very difficult, darling," Mum began. "It's about the company we own…"

"Yes," I said impatiently.

"Well, our company hasn't been doing too well recently and now we're going to have to close it down completely."

"For how long?" I asked.

"For good," Dad replied.

"But … but then what will I get for Christmas?" I asked.

Mum and Dad looked at each other.

"I'm sure we'll be able to manage something…" Dad began, but Mum interrupted him.

"We have to face facts, dear," she said to Dad. Then she turned to me. "Kathini, we're not sure we'll even be able to afford Christmas this year. We're going to have to move out of our house and we'll all have to tighten our belts."

"What does that mean?" I asked.

"We're going to have to make do. With everything we've got, we're going to have to use it up and wear it out," said Mum.

I looked at both of them. Dad bent his head. Mum sat with a stony expression on her face.

"You're joking – right?" I knew she wasn't but I had to ask anyway.

"We haven't got any money," Mum said, her voice as hard as stone. "We're going to have one gigantic sale and sell off all the toys and games we have left in our factory. If we sell enough we might just clear our debts but there'll be no money left over for luxuries – and Christmas is a luxury."

I jumped to my feet. "How could you? HOW COULD YOU?" I screamed at Mum and Dad. "I'm not going to have a proper Christmas and it's all your fault."

And I raced from the room, tears streaming down my face. After that, I barely spoke to Mum and Dad. We had all kinds of strangers tramping through our house, looking in my bedroom and all over. The fifth couple who came to look at our house said that they would buy it. I hated them too. How could they move into our house? Someone else would have *my* room. I cried and cried myself to sleep each night, but it didn't make any difference. Mum and Dad said they had to sell the house and that was that.

Mum and Dad decided to hold their toy sale on Christmas Eve, which was a Friday. They spent the days before Christmas Eve writing up lots of posters to advertise their sale. They put the ads all over the town where we lived.

In spite of all my wishing and hoping, Christmas Eve arrived far too soon. Mum and Dad were getting ready for their big toy sell-off.

"Come on, Kathini. Put on your coat and gloves," said Dad.

"No, I won't." I shook my head and crossed my arms. "I'm going to stay here."

"You can't stay here by yourself," Mum said firmly.

"Yes, I can," I argued.

"Kathini, you're going to come with us even if I have to carry you," said Mum. "This is hard enough on your dad and me as it is, without you making it ten times harder."

My eyes starting stinging when Mum said that, so to cover it up I scowled even harder. It was no use – Mum and Dad insisted that I had to help them sell all the toys and games they had left in their factory.

"I'm surprised you haven't asked me to sell all my toys as well," I sniffed.

"It might just come to that," Dad muttered.

I don't think I was meant to hear that bit, but I did.

Once we reached the warehouse, it took an hour for Mum and Dad to set everything up. All the toys Mum and Dad owned were set up on huge tables at the front of the building. Other grown-ups who worked at the factory were also there to help out, including Mr Johnson who's a good friend of my parents.

"What's the matter, Kathini? Why the long face?" he asked.

"It's not fair. I hope no one buys a thing," I sulked.

"Well, for your mum and dad's sake, I hope for once you *don't* get what you want," Mr Johnson replied, coldly.

Ignoring him, I sat on a chair behind one of the tables and watched as the gates were opened to the public. The tables were covered with a lot of toys I already had and some I didn't. Each toy had a price tag attached to it and I could see at once that most of the toys were less than half price.

It wasn't fair. It wasn't *right*. Where would all my toys come from in the future if Mum and Dad had to sell everything?

But half an hour later, I began to smile. We'd only had a few people on to the forecourt of the factory and only a couple of them had bought anything.

Let's hope no one else will turn up, I thought to myself.

And that's when I saw him – a boy, about my age. He wore tatty, patched trousers, a jumper with holes in it and a dirty anorak that wasn't zipped up. He wandered in my direction, his eyes huge as he took in everything on the table.

"This is amazing," he said when he'd reached me.

"Huh!" I answered.

"I wish I could afford just one thing here," he sighed. "Not for me, but for my brother."

"If you can't afford anything you should go away," I told him.

"I can at least look," he told me. "Looking is free."

I glowered at the boy, wishing he would leave.

"So what's your name?" the boy asked.

"Kathini." I didn't ask him what his name was. I thought he might get the hint from that – but he didn't.

"I'm Ileo," he smiled.

"That's a strange name. I've never heard that before," I couldn't help admitting.

"My dad said he chose it because it means 'I Love Everyone'," Ileo said proudly. "I like your name too. It's pretty. It suits you. Kathini…"

My face went all warm when he said that.

"Thanks," I smiled.

I don't know why but for the first time I noticed his clenched hands. He'd made fists against the icy weather in an effort to keep his fingers warm. The skin around his knuckles was pinched and wrinkled with the cold. I had on thick sheepskin mittens and I could still feel the Christmas chill. At that moment all I could think about was how uncomfortable his hands must be. My smile faded at the thought.

"What's the matter?" Ileo asked. He leaned forward, anxious to hear my reply. "You don't look very happy."

I didn't want to embarrass him by mentioning his hands so with a sigh, I pointed to the table in front of me.

"Mum and Dad – they have to sell all this stuff."

"Where did they get it all from?"

"They made it in their factory over there," I

replied. "But now they're having to sell the factory and these toys and our house 'cause they don't have any money."

"I'm sorry."

And Ileo really did look sorry too.

"So much for Christmas," I sniffed, fighting back the tears.

"What d'you mean?"

"We won't have any money to do *anything*," I said angrily. I would've thought it was obvious what I meant.

"What does Christmas mean to you then?" Ileo asked, surprised.

"Lots of presents, lots of food, staying up late, good things like that."

"No wonder you're so miserable," Ileo smiled. "You've got it all wrong."

"What d'you mean?"

"Christmas isn't about what you get. Christmas is about what you *give* – and I don't just mean things either."

"You can't give anything except things," I said, confused.

"Not true. You can give love, friendship, happiness. Things like that. Too many people think that all they need to make them happy is money and the things it can buy."

"Money does make people happy. If Mum and Dad had money we'd be happy now," I said.

"You think so?" Ileo asked me. "I bet your mum and dad worked so hard here that you didn't see them as often as you would've liked."

"They bought me lots of presents to make up for it."

"What would you rather have? Presents or your parents?"

I blinked with surprise. I'd never thought of it that way before.

"My dad says that too many people nowadays have forgotten how Christmas started and what it's really about," said Ileo.

"You mean that it's the day Jesus Christ was born?" I said doubtfully.

"But it's more than that. Imagine millions and millions of people all over the world celebrating one person's birthday – isn't that amazing!" said Ileo. "My dad says birthdays should be celebrated and enjoyed – not sweated over and cursed because they're so much expense and hard work. My dad says that was never what Christmas was meant to be about."

"I guess..." I hadn't really thought about that either.

"Anyway, I didn't mean to bend your ear." Ileo shrugged. "I'd better get home before everyone wonders where I've got to."

Ileo turned to leave. I looked around. Mum and Dad were nowhere in sight and the nearest grown-up was at least four tables away.

"Ileo, hang on. Would … would you like one of these toys?" I indicated the toys on the long table before me.

"Can't afford them," Ileo said cheerfully.

"You can take one if you'd like. You don't have to pay for it. Mum and Dad won't mind," I said.

"Are you sure?" Ileo raised his eyebrows.

I nodded. "Go ahead. Happy Christmas!"

Ileo picked up a model-making kit and hugged it to his chest.

"Great! Thanks! It's very kind of you. My brother will love it."

I started to grin at the look on Ileo's face. I couldn't help it. He was so happy. And the funny thing is – it seemed to rub off on me.

"Take something for yourself as well," I smiled.

"Are you sure?"

"Yeah! Go on."

"Are you sure you're sure?" Ileo asked, astounded.

"Go ahead. I want you to."

Ileo picked up another model-making kit, clutching it as if he'd never let it go.

I gasped with shock. "What's the matter with your hands?"

Ileo had an angry-looking scar on the back of each hand. I hadn't noticed them before but now I wondered how I could've missed them.

"The scars go all the way through – see!" Ileo raised one hand to show me his palm. The scar did indeed go all the way through to his palm.

"How did you do that? Does it hurt?" I asked, concerned.

"All the time," Ileo shrugged. "But I don't mind. I'd better get going. Just wait till my brother sees this! Not to mention my dad."

"Ileo, wait! Hang on a—" But it was too late. Off he raced. As I watched him go, I felt really strange. Yes, I was sad about the scars on his hands but he'd left me feeling … not just happy, but *glad* inside. It's hard to describe. It was like a light switching on inside me. That's the only way I can think of it.

"Are you OK, Kathini?" Dad appeared from

nowhere to stand beside me.

I smiled at him.

"Well, I'm glad to see you've cheered up a bit," Dad smiled. "I'm sorry about this. It's not going to be much of a Christmas for you I'm afraid."

"How're we doing?" I asked.

"Not very well," Dad sighed. "I think we're still going to have most of this stuff at the end of the day."

"And then what will happen to it?" I asked.

"The new owners of the factory will probably dump the lot. They're going to use the factory for something else so they don't want toys cluttering up the place," Dad explained.

"And if you sell all this stuff, will it get you and Mum out of trouble?" I asked.

"Not really. But we'll be able to have a decent Christmas. We'll be able to buy you lots of presents and we'll have lots of food. It'll be our best Christmas ever before we have to move house."

I took a look around. "But no one's here to buy any of it."

"I know." Dad's shoulders slumped as he too looked around.

"Dad, I know a way to get rid of it," I told him.

"How?"

"We could give it away," I said.

Dad stared at me. "Pardon?"

"Can we give it away, Dad?" I rushed on as Dad opened his mouth to argue. "No one's buying it anyway and lots of people would be glad of your toys. You make brilliant toys, Dad. So if we can't sell them, we could give them to people who really want them. Then they wouldn't end up on a rubbish dump somewhere."

"I … I don't know…"

Dad looked doubtful but I could see that he was having a serious think about it.

"Let me go and ask your mum," Dad said at last.

Five minutes later, Mum, Dad and all the other grown-ups were crowding around my table.

"I can't believe it!"

"Kathini, this was *your* idea?"

My face started to burn. For the first time, I actually listened to what they were saying. Before I heard what they were saying about me, but I didn't really listen – and because I didn't listen, I didn't take any notice. But now it was obvious what most of them thought of me. They thought I was selfish and spoilt and only thought about myself. And the worse thing was, they were absolutely right.

Mum smiled at me. "Would you really like us to give away these toys?" she asked.

I nodded, shyly.

"Well, I think that's a wonderful idea," said Dad.

"So do I," Mr Johnson agreed. He stared at me as if he couldn't quite believe that it had been my idea.

Mum said very softly, "Kathini, I'm proud of you."

And that's how we got our picture in the local newspaper.

We loaded up all the toys into large bin liners and set off to the shopping precinct. Whilst the grown-ups were wondering what to do next, I stepped forward and shouted at the top of my lungs, "Merry Christmas! Come and get some free toys. Merry Christmas!"

At first, not many people stopped. They must've thought it was a trick or something. But then one woman with her two children stopped, then a man with his son and soon we were surrounded and we couldn't give them away fast enough. But then two policemen arrived.

"Who's in charge here?" asked one of them.

Dad moved forwards.

"One of the toy shops in the precinct called us. You can't sell goods here without a licence," the policeman told him.

"I'm not selling these toys. I'm giving them away," Dad explained.

The policeman frowned at him. "If they're not safe, you can't give them away either."

"They're perfectly safe," said Dad. "They conform to all the rules and regulations regarding safe toys. We made them in our factory but as the factory is closing down for good in the New Year, we thought we'd give the toys away."

"That's very Christmassy of you!" said the other policeman.

Dad grinned at him. "We think so! It was all my daughter's idea."

And after that the two policemen helped us to give out the presents. Someone else must have called the local newspaper because within fifteen minutes we were all having our photographs taken. I've never had such a wonderful time. It was … magic! You should've seen the looks on people's faces when they got their toys. So many people came up to Mum and Dad and thanked them.

"I was wondering how I'd find the money to buy my son something for Christmas and now, thanks to you…"

"How can I ever thank you?" said another. "I just didn't have the money to buy toys this Christmas."

And as I watched the smiling faces all around us, it was like the light in me was burning brighter and brighter. It was such fun. Ileo was right.

When we got home that night, Mum and Dad were in a better mood than they'd been for a long time.

"Well, we didn't make a bean but I'm kind of glad," said Dad as he flopped down on to the sofa.

"It was good, wasn't it," Mum agreed. "At least we went out with a bang!"

Dad ordered a pizza and after we'd all eaten, I went to bed – for once without protesting about it. I had a lot to think about.

Christmas Day was sunny and bright. I looked out of my bedroom window over our back garden and it was as if I was seeing it for the first time. It was so beautiful. The bare trees waved gently in the wind. It was as if they were wishing me a good morning. I'd never noticed them before and now it was too late. I watched the trees for a long, long while. Then I had my shower and went down for breakfast.

"Happy Christmas, Kathini." Mum and Dad grinned at me as soon as I entered the living-room.

"Happy Christmas!" I replied. And I gave them both a kiss on the cheek.

"Open your present then," said Mum.

"I didn't think you'd bought me anything," I said, surprised.

"It's only small," Dad apologized.

"That doesn't matter," I smiled.

I opened my present. Usually for Christmas I got at least six or seven presents, but now I didn't mind that I'd only got one. And what a present it was! It was a dark purple jumper, covered with gold and silver embroidered stars. It was amazing, I put it on at once.

"And I've got something for both of you," I said slowly.

"What's that?"

"I want to say I'm sorry. I'm sorry that you've had to close down your factory and I'm sorry that I only thought about myself when you told me. I didn't mean to be such a brat." I felt like crying when I remembered all the horrible things I'd said and done. Looking back I couldn't believe it was the same person.

"What's brought all this about?" Mum asked me.

"Something Ileo said to me," I admitted.

"Who's Ileo?" Dad asked.

"The boy I was talking to yesterday at the factory, before we went to the precinct," I replied.

Dad frowned. "I didn't see you talking with any boy – and I was keeping an eye on you."

"You must have seen him. He was wearing old, worn-out clothes and his hair needed combing," I said.

"Kathini, your mum and I were keeping an eye on you all the time we were on the factory fore-court. We never saw you talk to anyone – except Mr Johnson," said Dad.

"You must've missed him then," I frowned. "It's a shame, because Ileo was so nice. I gave him a toy for himself and his brother."

"Good for you. And thank you, Ileo – whoever and wherever you may be," Mum smiled.

Mum, Dad and I had a wonderful Christmas. We played board games and stuffed our faces and cuddled up on the sofa to watch some films on the TV. I was so happy I couldn't stop smiling. None of us could. And that's when I knew that no matter what happened, as long as we were together, we'd be all right.

Well, since then, we've had our picture in the paper and then our story and picture appeared in a national newspaper and caused quite a stir. We were very popular with everyone but the owners of the toy shops in the precinct. And d'you know what happened in the New Year? Because of the picture in the paper, this man called Mr Gardner came to see my mum and dad. He said he'd like to go into partnership with them because they'd generated so much publicity that *everyone* wants our toys. Mum and Dad's factory was saved and we managed to keep our house.

Everything turned out OK in the end. So why do I call it my worst Christmas ever? Because it still makes me cringe to think about how I behaved before Christmas. It still makes my face burn to remember how much of a … a brat I was!

But I have changed. The only thing I wish now is that I could see Ileo again. I find I'm thinking about him a lot – every day. He said that Ileo stood for "I Love Everyone". I think that's wonderful. The strange thing is, I find myself talking to him in my head and I sometimes feel he actually talks back to me. It's as if we've always been friends and always will be. Isn't that strange? And isn't it sad that it took all the things that happened at Christmas for me to know him and to listen to him. But as I'm sure Ileo would say – better late than never. And do you know what the best thing about talking to Ileo in my head is? I'll tell you. When I talk to him I feel happy and every day is Christmas.

Mr Mackintosh

Aileen Paterson

When Mr Mackintosh came to help out at Lovett's Corner Shop, things were as bad as could be. Mrs Lovett was in hospital and Mr Lovett had gone down with a bad dose of 'flu. The weather had gone wrong too. It hadn't stopped raining for weeks.

It was Andy Lovett who'd suggested putting the notice in the window.

URGENT! TEMPORARY SHOP ASSISTANT REQUIRED FOR XMAS PERIOD. APPLY WITHIN.

"It's no good, Andy," said his dad. "It'll be a miracle if anyone wants a job so near Christmas. I can't pay much anyway."

But Andy wrote it out in his best writing and put it in the window. Somebody had to do something!

Things had been bad enough lately, with Mum in

hospital and Dad going round the bend trying to cope on his own. There was no one to help. His London grandma was away in Canada visiting her sister, and his Newcastle grandma had a job. Andy was very fed up. If his mum could see him, she'd give him a hug and say, "Cheer up, gloomyboots! You look like a wet weekend." But Mum wasn't here. It was difficult for his dad to get away from the shop so they could visit her every day. Andy missed her, and he was worried about her and the baby they were waiting for.

Andy missed Mum's cooking too. Dad made fish fingers and beans for tea *every* night. Fish fingers were fine, but not every night.

"They're coming out of my ears," he grumbled to his friend Gideon. "I'll be turning into a fish finger if this goes on."

"Some people might think that was an improvement," laughed his friend.

But now his dad was ill. When he got home from school, he'd found him sitting shivering in their flat at the back of the shop. Andy made him sit by the fire and fetched some aspirins and a cup of tea. Dad wanted to shut the shop, but Andy took his place behind the counter.

That was when he decided to put the notice in the window.

Looking out, he watched the rain pouring down. There was no one about. The rain was filling the gutters, swirling old crisp packets and matchsticks along in its path. Overhead some miserable starlings huddled together on the telephone wires. No one would have dreamt that it was nearly Christmas. The shop didn't look much better. His father seemed to have cancelled Christmas this year. The cards and wrapping paper were lying in a heap in a corner. He hadn't even put their own cards up in the flat.

Suddenly the shop bell began jangling noisily. The door flew open with a loud wharooshing noise, and a man stepped inside. He stopped halfway to the counter and stood there, looking around him.

Andy looked at the man. He was stocky with rosy cheeks and a pair of old-fashioned wire spectacles on his nose. He was wearing a raincoat and a long blue scarf with white stars all over it. Sandy curls stuck out from under his woolly hat. When he removed his hat off to shake the rain off, Andy noticed that he had a bald spot. One of his curls lay across it, like a piece of crispy bacon on a plate. He wasn't one of their regulars. Andy had never seen him before.

"Can I help you, sir?" asked Andy.

The man smiled.

"Funny, I was just going to ask you the same question! My name is Mackintosh. I've come to enquire about the job advertised in your window. Are you in charge here?"

Andy couldn't believe his ears. The notice had only been in the window for about five minutes, and already someone wanted the job.

"Er … I'm Andy Lovett," he stammered. "It's my dad's shop. He's in the back. Would you like to speak to him?"

The man nodded and followed Andy into the flat to meet Mr Lovett. Andy was dying to stay and see what happened but the shop bell rang again, so he got back to work. Ten minutes and three customers later, his father appeared with their visitor. They shook hands. Mr Mackintosh put on his woolly hat again and headed for the door.

"Cheerio!" he cried, waving to Andy. "See you both in the morning."

Then he was gone.

"Well, Andy," said his father. "You can take your advert out of the window. It did the trick. Mr Mackintosh is going to help us out till Christmas Eve. He seems a nice sort of chap. Used to have a little shop like ours up in Edinburgh. Let's hope he soon gets the hang of things here. Now, son, if you don't mind, I'm going to lock up and go to bed. I feel terrible. Can you make your own supper tonight? There's loads of fish fingers in the freezer."

"I know," said Andy.

In the morning his dad's 'flu was worse. Andy made him stay in bed then he telephoned for the doctor to come later. He was busy trying to eat some toast and bring in the milk crates and newspapers, when Mr Mackintosh arrived, and took over. Andy gave a sigh of relief. It was time to leave for school, and he could see Gideon waiting for him at the corner.

"Off you go, laddie," said Mr Mackintosh. "I'll take good care of your dad and the shop, I promise."

"Thanks," said Andy. "Bye, Dad."

It was only when he was halfway to school that he noticed that it wasn't raining. The sun had come out at last.

*   *   *

After school, Andy and Gideon walked home together. Gideon told him about his dad's new taxi, and about his granny. She had flown all the way from Jamaica to spend Christmas with them. He said she was a bit disappointed that there was no snow in London. She'd never seen snow. Andy said he wasn't sure there would be a proper Christmas in his house, with one thing and another.

When they reached the shop, Gideon said he'd see Andy in the morning, and headed home. Andy pushed open the shop door. He just stood and stared when he got inside. The floor was gleaming, the shelves had been dusted and tidied. The window was full of sweets and chocolates, and someone had painted snowflakes on the glass. There were red and gold Christmas decorations on the walls, and silver stars hanging from the ceiling. It was beautiful! And there was music playing. Not the music they had in the supermarket that his dad called tosh. No. This was like a faraway choir singing carols from long ago. *At last* Andy felt the tingle inside that comes when Christmas time is almost here.

Mr Mackintosh, dressed in a rainbow-striped jumper, was busy serving a queue of customers.

"Can I give you a hand?" asked Andy.

"Hello, Andy," said Mr Mackintosh. "I'm fine, thank you. I'm enjoying myself! Pop in and see your dad. He'll be pleased to see you."

"Righto. The shop looks great!"

The flat looked nice too. Their Christmas cards were hanging above the fireplace. A wonderful smell of cooking was coming from the kitchen. His dad was tucked up in bed reading. He looked much better.

"Hello," he said. "How was school?"

"Not bad. Quite good actually. We had a concert this afternoon. The headmaster did magic tricks, and Miss Miller did a tapdance!"

His dad smiled.

"Did the doctor come?"

"Yes. He said I was to stay in bed for a couple of days. Good job we have Mr Mackintosh to help. I phoned your mum to say we wouldn't be in to see her till I'm better. She's feeling fine, and she sends you her love."

Things were looking up, thought Andy. He felt happier than he had been for ages. Ever since Mr Mackintosh had arrived *everything* was better.

After the shop closed, it was time for supper. It was a lot better than usual too. Mr Mackintosh was a good cook. He said he had never heard of fish fingers. He didn't know fish had any! Instead they all had chicken stew and baked potatoes, and apple crumble to follow. It was delicious.

Mr Mackintosh was full of surprises!

There were more next day.

"I've got a job for you," said Mr Mackintosh when Andy got home. There, in the sitting-room, stood a Christmas tree in a red tub.

"It's just a wee present from me. Christmas isn't Christmas without a tree," he said, handing Andy a box of ornaments and lights.

"I'm sure you'll manage to make it look bonny, and we can put all your parcels underneath."

"PARCELS?" said Andy.

"Yes. Parcels. Didn't I mention it? The postman's delivered a big pile of them for you all."

Andy enjoyed decorating the tree all by himself. Besides the ornaments and fairy lights, there were little toys and chocolate teddy bears. He tied them all carefully on to the branches, then last of all there was a big glittering star for the top. Mr Mackintosh came in from the shop with loads of gaily wrapped parcels, and they put them all around the tree. Last of all, Andy switched off the light in the room and Mr Mackintosh switched on the tree lights… Andy's dad came through in his dressing-gown to watch. It was the twinkliest, best Christmas tree any of them had ever seen!

The day after that was *full* of good things. It was the last day of school before the holidays, and each class had a party. When the school bell rang, Andy and Gideon raced out of the gates, and there, parked outside, was Gideon's dad's taxi.

"Special orders from Mr Mackintosh!" said Gideon's dad. When they arrived at the shop, Andy's dad was waiting for him. He was better at last. He was even dressed in his coat and scarf.

"Let's go, Andy," he said. "Your mum phoned. The baby is on its way!"

Gideon and Mr Mackintosh waved to them till the taxi disappeared.

It was late when they got back. Mr Mackintosh put their supper in the oven and waited for them. At last the flat door flew open.

"It's a *boy!*" cried Andy and his dad. "And they're both fine."

"Tell me all about it."

"He's got a loud voice," laughed Andy. "And he's got red hair like me, and he's strong. He wouldn't let my finger go!" His eyes were shining with happiness.

"He sounds just terrific," said Mr Mackintosh. "I like new babies. They look just like a dumpling in a hankie. Has he got a name yet?"

"Mum says we're to call him after you, for coming to help us at Christmas. What's your name?"

Mr Mackintosh went very red, and blew his nose. "That's the nicest Christmas present I've ever had. My name is Noel."

"Then our baby is Noel Lovett!" said Andy and his dad.

On Christmas Eve it was time for Mr Mackintosh to go. He had done his job and now it was over. He said goodbye to all the Lovett family. Mrs Lovett was home again with the baby. Mr Mackintosh had put presents for everyone under the tree, and Andy handed him his present.

"Thank you for everything, from all of us. Please come back and see us again. We're going to miss you."

"I'll do my best," smiled Mr Mackintosh. "Merry Christmas, Andy."

He waved goodbye to them all and walked up the street. There were snowflakes drifting in the wind. Mr Mackintosh caught one in his hand. Gideon's granny won't be disappointed, he thought. He thought of them all waking up tomorrow to a white Christmas. He thought of the new baby. "That's what Christmas is all about," he said to himself.

He climbed to the top of the hill and looked back at Lovett's Corner Shop. Everything had gone well. If it hadn't been for Andy, he would never have had the chance to come and help. He put his hand in his raincoat pocket and took out the present Andy had given him. When he unwrapped it, he laughed. It was a harmonica! He put it in his mouth and began to play. The snow swirled round him as his hat and scarf and raincoat dissolved and changed into a long gown of shimmering white. His wings unfolded and lifted in the night wind. Mr Mackintosh, still playing, rose into the air and flew up through the snowclouds into the blue sky of Heaven.

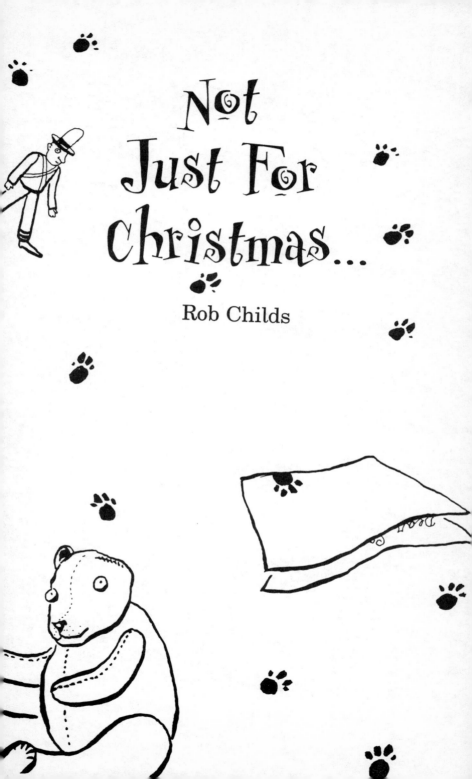

Not Just For Christmas...

Rob Childs

J ames woke up very early with an extra special sense of excitement.

"Christmas Day!" He felt like shouting it out. He had been looking forward to this day for so long, and now – at last – it was here!

Trembling, James sat up in bed and rubbed his eyes. He opened them again, slowly, but everywhere was dark and he still couldn't see anything.

He tried not to be too disappointed. "Maybe they're with all my other presents," he murmured. "Santa must have been by now."

James liked to talk to himself, to hear the sound of his voice in the darkness. He was glad he had his own bedroom. It was his private little world, a place where he knew that nobody else would be nearby to listen. Like Hannah, for instance.

His sister was OK to play with at times, he admitted, but she was only five, three years younger than him. Her never-ending chatter often irritated him, especially if she got too big for her boots and tried to do things for him.

"I wonder where everything will be this year?" he said aloud.

It was part of the family fun at Christmas. After Santa's visit, Mum and Dad would hide the presents all over the house and then go back to sleep. He and Hannah had to wait, bursting with anticipation, until their parents said they could start looking. James considered whether he might risk going to wake them up yet so he could begin the hunt.

"Bet it's still a bit too early."

He reached under the pillows instead for his favourite toy soldier, but his fingers first touched a piece of paper. It was a copy of his letter to Santa, put there for safe keeping, and he gave it a superstitious pat.

Then his hand closed around the small plastic figure with a gun and he whipped it out with a flourish. "Bang!" he cried, pretending to shoot at the one-eared teddy bear that lay by his side. "Bang! Bang!"

He chuckled as Teddy had to dive down on to the carpet to escape the bullets. James leapt out of bed after him and the fight went on as Sam the soldier chased Teddy across the floor.

"Oooh! It's too cold!" James said, with a shiver. He grabbed Teddy and scrambled back under the duvet, wriggling right down until he was completely covered. Snuggling up with Teddy, he felt warm again and happy, hoping it wouldn't be long before he'd be able to see all the pretty lights on the Christmas tree. He closed his eyes and crossed his fingers.

"James! James! Wake up!"

He was being pushed and pulled about, but he stayed underneath the thick duvet out of sight.

"I *am* awake," came his muffled voice. "Go away!"

"You were fast asleep," Hannah insisted. "I was awake before you."

His tousled head shot out from the covers. "No, you weren't. I've been awake for years."

"No, you haven't! I was up first this morning."

"Rubbish! I even helped Santa empty his sack!"

Hannah gave up. She could never win such silly arguments with her stubborn big brother.

"It's time!" she announced instead.

James knew exactly what she meant. "I know,"

he replied. "I was just waiting for you, that's all, so we went in together."

She gave him a funny look, but knew that all the faces she might pull were just wasted on James. "Come on, then. Let's go in!"

Tingling with excitement, the children crept along the landing and pushed open the door to their parents' bedroom.

"Dad's snoring," James hissed.

"Goodie!" giggled Hannah. "We can both sneak up on him and make him jump!"

James felt his sister's hand slide into his as they tiptoed into the room towards Dad's side of the bed.

"Oh no, you don't, you two!" came a voice in the darkness. "I know what you're up to!"

"Mummy!" Hannah squealed. "Oh, you spoiled it!"

Mum laughed. "You little pests. Do you know what time it is?"

"No," said James, "but I do know what day it is. It's Christmas Day!"

"Come on in," Mum invited them, drawing back the duvet covers. "Come and have a Christmas cuddle."

Hannah slithered in first for a kiss from Mum, quickly followed by James. Dad rolled over. "Who's the elephant with cold feet?" he grumbled sleepily.

"James, Daddy!" Hannah cried. "Happy Christmas!"

"Christmas is cancelled!"

"No, it's not!" they chorused.

"Yes, it is," he said. "Haven't you heard? Santa's gone on holiday!"

"No, he hasn't. You're just teasing," James chuckled, punching Dad on the shoulder. "He only goes on holiday after he's delivered all our presents. It's time now."

"It's time, Mummy," echoed Hannah. "It's time!"

"I can see we're not going to get any peace," Mum said. "OK, it's time. Off you go while I make a drink."

The children whooped their delight and shot out of the bed, desperate to be the one to find the first present. They always knew whose it was by the wrapping. Hannah's gifts had ribbon around them and a bow, while James's were tied up loosely with string. He loved pulling off the string and tearing open the packaging to see what was inside.

"Found one straight away!" he screamed proudly

as he squirmed underneath the bed. "And it's mine!"

He ripped the string and wrapping paper away from the box and held it up to his nose. "Hmm, yummy smell! My favourite chocs!"

His next discovery, at the bottom of a wardrobe, didn't have anything round it at all. It didn't need it. James knew what it was as soon as he felt around the shoes and touched it. "Wow! A football. Thanks!"

Dad laughed. "Santa would have had a terrible job trying to wrap up a football! He obviously didn't bother."

James stopped searching for anything else for a while, dribbling the ball around the bedroom with his bare feet and knocking into things as he lost control.

"Hey! Steady on, superstar," cried Dad, getting out of bed himself at last. "You'll go and break something and then we'll all be in trouble. Let's wait till we get outside in the garden later."

Shrieks and squeals from Hannah confirmed her own successes, and the children spent a very happy hour up and down the stairs, poking and probing into cupboards and drawers. James even found a tape of one of his best-loved stories lying in the bath.

"Good job I didn't turn the taps on first," he grinned.

Mum laughed. "No danger of you volunteering to have a bath, is there, you mucky pup."

She caught Dad's eye and they smiled at what she had just said. Mum put down her cup of tea and pulled the two children gently towards her on the sofa.

"Uncle John is coming round later this morning," she said, giving them both a hug. "He's bringing along something else for you, although it's not really a Christmas present. It's something even more special."

Hannah's eyes widened. "Is it a pony?" she gasped.

Mum shook her head and smiled. "No guessing allowed. We want it to be a surprise."

Mum supervised their washing and dressing while Dad prepared some breakfast. "What time is Uncle John coming?" asked Hannah the moment she trotted into the kitchen.

"Soon," Dad said. "You'll have to be patient and play with all your new toys until he gets here."

"Will we be able to play with what he's bringing?" she persisted.

"Still trying to work out what it can be, aren't you?" he laughed. "But yes, you'll certainly be able to play with it."

James was strangely quiet at the table, nibbling at a piece of toast, and Dad attempted to cheer him up. "How about us two going out to kick your new ball about a bit, eh?"

James nodded, but didn't look up. "Have I found *all* my presents yet?" he asked instead.

"Not quite," Mum replied. "I think there are still a couple of things hidden away."

"I'll help him look for them," Hannah piped up.

"No you won't!" cried James. "I don't need any help. I'll find them when I'm ready."

Hannah was about to answer him back until Mum shot her a warning glance and she swiftly changed the subject. "This is the best Christmas ever," she beamed. "I've got everything I wanted. Have you, James?"

"Not yet," he said simply and slid away from the table to play with the toy cars that he'd left near the fire.

When the bell rang, the children rushed to the

door, both wanting to be the one to open it. Hannah won the race – as usual.

"Hi, kids!" Uncle John greeted them. "Merry Christmas, everyone!"

Hannah looked all around for whatever it was that Uncle John was supposed to have with him. There was nothing to be seen.

"Did you like my presents I got Santa to leave for you?" he asked and then laughed at their blank expressions. "Just like me when I was your age. Too busy opening the boxes to bother with the labels!"

"Uncle John bought you those horrible noisy, electronic games," Dad explained, slipping his younger brother a wink. "Typical! He won't be the one who's got to put up with all the din every time you play with them."

"Oh, thank you, Uncle John!" Hannah said politely as he picked her up to give her a peck on the cheek.

"Thanks, I'll have some fun with that, annoying Dad," grinned James.

Uncle John acted as though he'd just remembered something. "Oh, yes, I almost forgot. There's another thing you'll have a lot of fun with, too. I've left it in the car."

Still carrying Hannah, he led the way out on to the drive, and his niece suddenly let out a shriek. From her high vantage point, she could see into the back of his estate car. "A puppy! A real puppy!"

She squirmed out of his grasp and ran to the car to stare through the rear window. "Oh, it's beautiful. It's so cute. What big eyes!"

"It's a *she*," Uncle John said. "And she's not so cute when she leaves little puddles all over your carpet and inside your car!"

The children laughed and demanded the car be open so that they could hold the puppy.

"Thanks for looking after her for a couple of days, John," Mum said. "Hope she hasn't been too much trouble to you."

"None at all," he grinned. "Apart from the puddles!"

"What is she?" asked James.

"A labrador," said Dad. "And she's just seven weeks old."

James stroked the puppy's short, stubby nose and chin as Hannah cuddled her. "What shall we call her?" he wondered.

"Actually, she's already got a name," said Mum. "It's Misty."

"Who gave her that?"

"The people at the kennels where she was born."

James considered it for a moment. "OK, Misty's a fine name."

Mum smiled with relief. "Do you like her?" she asked anxiously.

He nodded. "I've often wanted a dog to play with."

"I know, but we weren't quite sure if it would be a good thing," Dad said. "Especially after that big dog down the street knocked you over."

"It wasn't the dog's fault," James said. "I must have stepped on its tail or something and hurt it."

"You cried," gloated his sister. "I remember you crying."

"So?" he demanded. "You would have done too. You're always crying. It just made me jump, that's all. I didn't know what was happening."

"Anyway, never mind now, don't argue," Mum said, prising the puppy out of Hannah's arms. "Let James hold Misty for a while, darling."

Hannah looked down at her dress in dismay. "Oh! I'm all wet!"

Everyone laughed. "Serves you right for squeezing her so tight," Dad chuckled.

"Let's take Misty into the back garden and play ball," said James as Mum led Hannah into the house to change her clothes.

His new football was far too big for the puppy and James kicked a small ball across the lawn instead. It was ideal. The ball made a rattling sound as it rolled along, attracting her attention, and Misty scampered after it with yelps of excitement.

Dad and Uncle John joined in the game, laughing at the puppy's antics. The ball was just the right size for Misty and light enough for her to nose it through the grass in a wayward dribble. Dad passed the rattling ball to James who timed his next kick perfectly, sending it flying into the bushes by the fence.

"Goal!" cried Uncle John. "Great stuff, James. We'll have you playing for United yet."

"Rovers!" James corrected him. "They're the best team in the land."

The puppy soon grew weary. She squatted on the lawn and then settled down for a nap.

"Dog-tired! Just like the Rovers' players," joked Uncle John to tease James again about his favourite football team.

Dad carried Misty inside for a drink of water

from the shiny metal bowl that his brother had also brought with him. She lapped noisily at the water, spilling most of it on to the kitchen floor.

"Looks like we'll get through a lot of newspapers, soaking up all her messes," Mum chuckled. "I just hope Misty realizes what a lucky puppy she is, coming to live with us until she grows up."

"Till she grows up?" repeated James in alarm. "What do you mean?"

Mum put her arm around his shoulders and led him through to the lounge, calling Hannah to join them. As the family sat together near the Christmas tree, Misty curled up asleep on the rug in front of the fire.

"Misty doesn't know it yet," Mum said, "but when she's older and specially trained, she's going to have a very important job to do."

"What's that?" James interrupted impatiently, but the answer stunned him into silence.

"She will become a guide dog for a blind person."

Dad picked up the story. "But while she's a puppy, she needs to be looked after and loved just like any normal pet. That's where we come in. We've decided to be puppy-walkers."

"Puppy-walkers!" giggled Hannah. "What a

funny name!"

"Perhaps it is," Mum smiled, "because we'll be doing far more than just walking Misty. She'll be one of the family for a whole year."

"But then has she got to go to somebody else?" asked James.

"I'm afraid so," Dad answered. "But we can always take on another puppy after that, if we want to."

"We thought it might be better this way at first," Mum explained. "Just to let you get used to having a dog around the house. See how you get on together."

"We'll get on just fine," he said seriously. "I've never heard of people being puppy-walkers. It's a good idea."

James lay down next to the puppy on the rug, stroking her soft fur and gently fondling her large, floppy ears. He was rewarded with little grunts of contentment, almost like purring, and then felt his hand being licked by a rasping, wet tongue.

"Ooh! It tickles!" he chuckled.

Hannah didn't intend to be left out. She wanted to be licked too, and Misty rolled her tongue along the girl's bare arm as far as she could reach, sending Hannah into fits of giggles.

"Misty certainly won't be going short of love and fuss here, I can see that," Uncle John laughed. "She's fallen on her feet all right – and she knows it!"

As the puppy dozed, Hannah disappeared to try on her new ballet costume, but James stayed at Misty's side, his hand resting on one of her stretched out legs. "She feels so warm," he murmured happily.

"You look wonderful together, lying there," Mum told him. "We'll have to take a photo of you both like that."

There was no chance now. Misty was awake again – and looking for a spot of mischief. She found a willing partner in James, equally eager to play and tumble about.

"Here you are," said Dad. "Have one of my old socks to play tug-of-war with. Dogs love that game."

"Hope it's a clean one and not too smelly," laughed James, who soon felt a determined tugging at the other end of the sock.

"Misty doesn't seem to mind, anyway," Dad grinned.

James let Misty win some of the battles, but she

always brought the sock straight back, nudging him to grab hold of it again. Then he decided to throw it away for her to fetch.

The sock landed right on top of the Christmas cake on the table.

"Good job your mum didn't see that!" cried Uncle John, lifting it off quickly and returning it to James. "Try again."

He did, and this time it went into the trifle!

"I think you're better at kicking than throwing," said Uncle John.

The sock came back with a little trace of cream which Misty soon found. She licked her lips with pleasure at the taste.

James played with Misty almost all day in between her frequent snoozes and feeding times. He even forgot to search for his remaining presents until just before bedtime. He wanted Misty to sleep in his bedroom with him as well, but Mum had to be very firm about that.

"She's better off in the kitchen," Mum said. "She needs a place of her own at night too, just like you. And I can put plenty of newspaper all over the floor there around her dog basket!"

Mum sat on the side of his bed and read him a

story. "Have you enjoyed having a puppy to play with?" she asked, before saying good night.

James nodded several times. "We're going to have great fun, Misty and me, while she's with us. I can teach her lots of things."

"Yes, like how to get into all sorts of trouble, no doubt," Mum laughed. "And how to get all mucky!"

"Can I have a dog of my own one day?"

"Of course. When you're older. You'll be able to go everywhere together then."

James grinned. "I'll call mine Sam."

"Why Sam?"

James shrugged, unwilling to admit to his soldier's name. "I just like the sound of it."

Mum bent over to kiss him and caught sight of a piece of paper sticking out from underneath his pillow. She guessed what it was. James had insisted on having a copy of the letter she'd written to Santa for him. Mum remembered off by heart the words that he'd wanted her to write, but she couldn't resist the temptation to read them again now.

Mum quietly slid the paper away from the pillow without James realizing what she was doing. He lay with a happy, peaceful expression on his face, his eyes closed.

A few silent tears escaped from hers as she read over the short letter:

Dear Santa,

I hope you are well. My name is James and I am eight years old. Please can I have a new pair of eyes at Christmas? I keep bumping into things. I know this will be difficult, but I'm sure you will find a way of doing it somehow.

Thank you very much.

Love James

P.S. It would even be nice to see my pesky little sister as well.

Mum slipped the paper back into place and kissed James again. That lovely picture of him lying cosily beside Misty in the glow of the fire swam into her mind. "I'm so glad you like your new pair of eyes, my darling," she whispered.

He smiled and his eyes flickered open, staring up at her blindly.

Author's note:

The Guide Dogs for the Blind Association run puppy-walking schemes in many parts of the country. Families take a puppy, usually a labrador or a golden retriever, into their home to rear as an ordinary pet for the first year of its life. The young dog then goes to stay at a special training centre to learn how to become a guide dog, but a blind person needs to be at least sixteen before they can own one.

Kookaburra Christmas

Herbie Brennan

While he was going walkabout on Christmas Eve, Cheekyfella Tabagee found a baby by a billabong.

The little fella was lying in a basket. He had no clothes on, but somebody had stuck a big fern into the ground to give him shade.

All the same, it was no place to leave a youngster. Dingoes came down to the billabong to drink and there were snakes and spiders with poison in their mouths.

"Where are your folks, little fella?" Cheekyfella asked. He looked around for tracks in the grass and in the bush, but there was nothing. It was as if the baby had been set down from the sky.

Cheekyfella reached into the basket and lifted the baby out. The little fella looked at him with soft brown eyes and gurgled. His skin was lighter than Cheekyfella's dusty black, but darker than the white folks at the saw mill. He had the wizened, old-man look that meant he was brand new – hour or two at the most.

"What are we going to do with you, Cheekyfella asked. He grinned at the bab, baby grinned right back at him.

Cheekyfella waited a while in case the b. folks came back. No snakes slithered by, but couple of dingoes came sniffing round. They looked mean and hungry and would have taken the baby if Cheekyfella hadn't been there.

From where he squatted by the basket, Cheekyfella watched the sky turn red as the sun went down. He got to feeling peckish, so he dug round some roots until he found a witchetty and popped it in his mouth.

The little fella watched him with interest.

"Can't give you one," Cheekyfella said. "You're too young." Which was true enough, but trouble. Although the little fella hadn't cried yet, he was bound to want milk soon.

When it got to be dark, Cheekyfella knew he couldn't leave the baby lying there much longer. He stared at the stars and thought a while. Then he picked up the basket and trotted off into the bush.

*   *   *

Mabel Stiga went a bit peculiar when she lost her baby. She didn't exactly leave the tribe, but she took to living on her own. She'd have nothing to do with her husband any more and he finally went off to work in Alice. She heard Cheekyfella coming before she saw him.

"You bring me any tucker, Cheekyfella?" she called into the darkness beyond her camp fire.

Cheekyfella stepped into the firelight carrying a basket. He was a thin boy, maybe nine years old. Just now he was wearing khaki shorts that had seen better days. "Not this time, Mabel. Brought you a baby to mind, though."

Mabel's eyes shone as she looked into the basket. "Why, he's lovely, Cheekyfella. Where did you get him?"

"Somebody left him by the billabong. Dunno where he came from before that."

Mabel wasn't listening. She had lifted the baby out of the basket and was making silly noises at it. The little fella looked into her broad black face and beamed.

"See that, Cheekyfella – he likes me!" Mabel said. She turned back to the little fella and cooed,

"Got to get you fed, young fella. Got to get you fed."

"You do that, Mabel," Cheekyfella said. He started to move off.

"Where you going, Cheekyfella?" Mabel asked him.

"Gotta get my beauty sleep," Cheekyfella said. He nodded towards the baby in Mabel's arms. "I have to find his folks tomorrow."

Cheekyfella woke before the sun came up so he was back beside the billabong at dawn. He saw at once that somebody had been here. The fern was missing and there were tracks.

Cheekyfella studied them carefully. His Pa, Joe Tabagee, taught him always to look first. That way you knew what you were hunting before it turned and ate you.

The ground was mussed about a bit. There were signs of dingo, wallaby and 'roo. There was even the flat-footed print of a big croc. Cheekyfella shivered to think what it would have done with the little fella if Cheekyfella hadn't taken him.

But in amongst it all were man-tracks. The feet were too big for a woman, although the tracks were very light. Cheekyfella trotted off to follow them.

After a while it struck him he was heading towards a sandstone outcrop known as Carpet Snake Rock. Ghosts and spirits hung out at Carpet Snake Rock, which was a sacred place right back to the Dreamtime. Only Clever Men dared go there.

Cheekyfella kept on going, hoping the man he was following would turn aside. But the tracks said he was moving straight as a crow. Before he knew it, Carpet Snake Rock hove into sight.

He slowed, still hoping the man had turned aside, but after ten minutes more he knew he was in trouble. The tracks led right up to Carpet Snake Rock. Worse still, they seemed to be heading for Dead Man's Cave.

Cheekyfella strained his eyes. There was a light in Dead Man's Cave.

Cheekyfella squatted down and rubbed his chin. Not even Clever Men went into Dead Man's Cave. All the most powerful ghosts and spirits gathered there. It was more than a man's life was worth to go in, day or night.

Except one man had gone in – the man Cheekyfella was tracking.

Somebody had to warn him. As well as tell him that his baby was all right.

Cheekyfella stood up and trotted on. He felt afraid, but he knew it wouldn't do him any good so he ignored it.

As he started to climb Carpet Snake Rock, he could feel the spirits gathering all around him. He ignored that too.

There was a rocky apron to the front of Dead Man's Cave. Squatting on it was a Clever Man named Scratching Woman. He was doing something with a set of bones.

"G'day, Cheekyfella," he said without looking up.

"G'day, Scratch," Cheekyfella said. "What you doing with the bones?"

Scratch sniffed loudly. "Threw them to find out if the next fella to go into Dead Man's Cave would live to tell the tale."

Cheekyfella glanced towards the cave. It looked like somebody had an electric light switched on in there. "What did the bones tell you, Scratch?"

Scratching Woman frowned. "Don't rightly know," he said. "Sometimes with the bones it's hard to say."

Cheekyfella squatted down beside him. "I found

a baby, Scratch," he said. "I think that must be his pa in there."

Scratch shook his head. "Don't think so, Cheekyfella. What you got in there's an angel."

Cheekyfella frowned. "How do you know that, Scratch?"

Scratching Woman shrugged. "That light's coming from his face. Ghosts and spirits don't shine much, so it's got to be an angel."

Cheekyfella thought about it for a moment. "What's an angel look like?" he asked curiously.

"Didn't get a look at this one," Scratching Woman said. "But most of them are much what you'd expect – wings, white suit, Holy Joe expression. Look a bit like Yankee preachers."

Cheekyfella thought about it some more. "So you don't think it's got anything to do with the baby, Scratch?"

Scratch scooped the bones and dropped them in his tucker bag. "Didn't say that. I just don't reckon the angel is his pa."

"So what do you reckon?"

Scratch stretched and stood up. "I reckon that's the angel who delivers special babies every Christmas. Old tradition started out in Bethlehem."

"How special is special?" Cheekyfella asked.

Scratching Woman fixed him with a gimlet eye. "*Very* special, Cheek," he said.

Cheekyfella Tabagee and Scratching Woman trotted through the bush.

"I still reckon I should have gone into that cave and told the angel I was the one took his special baby," Cheekyfella said.

"He'd have killed you," Scratching Woman said. "Can't trust anybody who looks like a Yankee preacher."

"But you're sure we can make it right?"

"I reckon," Scratching Woman said. "Get the little fella up to Carpet Snake Rock, leave him outside Dead Man's Cave and whistle. Time the angel comes to see who's whistling, we'll be long gone. Angel gets his special baby back. Nobody gets hassled. Perfect plan."

But it wasn't a perfect plan. Mabel Stiga wouldn't give the baby back.

"He *likes* me!" she said, staring defiantly at Scratch and Cheekyfella. "He *wants* to stay with me!"

"You don't know that," Scratch said. "He's too

young to tell you what he wants."

"He smiles at me," said Mabel. "He smiles at me all the time."

"That's just wind," Scratch told her patiently.

"The baby belongs to an angel, Mabel," Cheekyfella put in.

"Then what's it doing leaving him beside a billabong?" snapped Mabel angrily. "Dingoes go down there to drink."

Cheekyfella thought she had a point. But he had to get the baby back. "Mabel," he said, "Scratch tells me that's a very special baby. Angels deliver one to somebody each Christmas. Been doing it for years, way back to baby Jesus. This one's late already."

"Where's the angel delivering him?" asked Mabel.

"Sydney ... Canberra..." said Cheekyfella vaguely. "Maybe London or New York."

Mabel sniffed. "White folks," she said. She glared at Scratch and Cheekyfella. "How come the white folks always get the special babies?"

Cheekyfella said, "I don't rightly know where he *is* going. Maybe it's not to the white folks."

But the damage was done. Mabel moved to

stand between them and the baby. "You touch that little fella over my dead body."

Dead or alive, her body was huge. Scratch and Cheekyfella backed off.

"What we going to do now, Scratch?" Cheekyfella asked as they trotted slowly through the bush.

"Reckon you're going to have to explain the problem to the angel," Scratch told him.

Cheekyfella hung back from the cave mouth. "Thought you said he'd kill me if I went in."

"Figure of speech," Scratch said. "You got more chance being eaten by a croc than killed by an angel."

"So you reckon I'll be all right?" Cheekyfella asked uncertainly. There was a woman eaten by a croc just two weeks ago.

"Right as rain," Scratch told him confidently even though it hadn't rained in the Outback for the past five years.

Cheekyfella entered Dead Man's Cave clutching Scratch's tucker bag for luck.

The angel was sitting on a rock, wearing a white suit. His wings were folded and the light from his face had died down so it didn't hurt to look at him. He was a little fella with big feet. He didn't look much older than Cheekyfella himself.

"G'day, angel," Cheekyfella said politely. He felt relieved the angel looked so young. The feet were sort of reassuring too.

"G'day," the angel answered bleakly. "Suppose you've come about the baby?"

Cheekyfella blinked. "Matter of fact…"

"It wasn't my fault!" the angel said at once. "The directions were really stupid."

Cheekyfella couldn't take his eyes off the wings. They were shimmery and hazy as if they weren't quite there, not like a bird's wings at all. "Directions?" he asked blankly.

The angel looked about to cry. "This is my first time in Australia. In fact it's my first time altogether on the Christmas baby run. I got lost."

"That why you left the baby by the billabong?" Cheekyfella asked.

"I only meant to leave it for a minute," the young angel told him earnestly. "He was getting nervous because I'd been flying round in circles. I thought if I could find a landmark I'd be OK. But then I couldn't find my way back to the baby."

"It happens," Cheekyfella told him sympathetically. White folks were always getting lost in the bush. Nobody had ever taught them to read the signs.

The angel looked desolate. "I got back to the billabong in the middle of the night. But by then he'd gone."

"Yeah, I know," Cheekyfella said. "I—"

"So what's my punishment?" the angel asked.

Cheekyfella blinked. "Punishment?"

There was a moment's silence in the cave. Eventually the angel said, "Haven't you been sent to punish me? By—?" He glanced upwards and jerked his head meaningfully towards the ceiling of the cave. "You know."

"Nothing like that," Cheekyfella said. "I just came to tell you I found the baby."

The angel jumped down off the rock. "You've found him! Is he all right?"

"Right as rain," said Cheekyfella without thinking.

"Where is he?" asked the angel looking round. "Did you bring him?"

Cheekyfella took a deep breath. "Bit of bother there," he said. The angel's face was flickering like a faulty light. Cheekyfella reckoned it must be the upset. "I *tried* to bring him here," he started to explain.

But the angel cut across him. "I have to get him back right now," he said. "Mrs Stiga should have had him *last night*! He's hours late already."

"Who?" asked Cheekyfella quickly.

"Mrs Mabel Stiga," said the angel. "The baby was supposed to go to Mrs Mabel Stiga."

The light inside was fading as Cheekyfella walked out of Dead Man's Cave.

"Get it sorted?" Scratching Woman asked him.

"Piece of cake," said Cheekyfella cheerfully. "Let's go tell Mabel she can keep the baby."

Together they started down from Carpet Snake Rock.

The
Christmas
Squirrel

Philippa Gregory

Redan the squirrel woke with a little squirm of hunger in his fat tummy. As soon as his eyes opened, they closed again and he fell asleep. It was like this every day in autumn and winter. He would wake on sunny warm days, find his store of acorns or pine nuts and have a picnic in the high branches of the trees. But on cold, wet and windy days he would turn around, clasp his warm tail closer with his little paws, fall fast asleep and dream of food.

The sun came out from behind the cold white winter clouds. It warmed Redan's glossy red fur. He opened a dark inquisitive eye and peeped out of his winter nest.

Below him were two children and their father, walking through the wood. The father was carrying a spade, the children were running beside him and around him, their big red feet making prints in the white frost.

Funny fur, Redan thought, looking at their bright red anoraks. And funny feet too. He leaned out of his dray to see better. A robin landed on a nearby branch.

"What's going on?" Redan asked.

"Christmas," the robin replied. This robin thought he knew everything about people. All summer long he would perch on garden fences, even hopping towards the people when they were digging in the flower bed in case they turned up a little worm or two. In winter he was first on the squirrel table, first at the peanuts. Redan had said a few words to him about hanging around the squirrel table and stealing squirrel food.

"It's a bird table," the robin had said. "For feeding birds."

This just showed how little the robin understood, Redan thought. Why would anyone want to feed birds? Of course not. People made these little tables, put out crumbs of bread, and hung nets of peanuts for squirrels. For the comfort and convenience of squirrels. Why else?

"Is Christmas something for squirrels?" he asked.

The robin made a squawk of disdain. "Of course not," he said scornfully. "It's something people do.

They chop down a tree and take it into the house. They put it in a big pot and hang it with lights and sparkly balls and sometimes silver-wrapped chocolates."

"For squirrels?"

"No," the robin said impatiently. "I've told you. For themselves. Their fledglings like it. And then on Christmas morning a wonderful thing happens. Under the tree they find a whole heap of brightly wrapped, beautiful…"

"Squirrels!" exclaimed Redan.

The robin laughed so much he nearly fell off the twig.

"Presents," he said. "Toys and things to eat, and things to play with. Squirrels don't come into it. Squirrels have nothing to do with it."

Redan looked surprised. "Then it can't be very important," he said.

The robin laughed and flew ahead of the people, watching to see which way they would go.

Redan let him go and stretched out his strong legs and his little paws. He was hungry again. He had a very clear memory of a little store of nuts that he had left under an oak tree. He skipped out of his dray and scampered from one tree to another, till he came to the oak tree.

There was nothing there.

Redan chattered softly to himself. Someone must have stolen his store of nuts. This was the second time it had happened this winter. It might even be the third or the fourth time – he couldn't remember very well. But he thought it might be the robin stealing his food.

He had another store in a fir tree, deeper in the wood. He swarmed up the trunk of the oak tree and then danced from branch to branch over the heads of the people, to the fir tree. He scampered down the trunk of the tree to where an old woodpecker's nest made a good hiding-place for nuts. Nothing there either. Nothing left but a few empty shells.

The robin arrived and folded his wings, in the smug way which robins have.

"Look, have you had my nuts?" Redan demanded. "Because if you have been following me around, finding my stores, eating my nuts then I'll..."

The robin hitched up his wing. "Do I look like I could crack nuts?" he asked, looking down his tiny narrow beak.

Redan hesitated. "Squirrels can," he said.

"I know," the robin said. "But robins can't. I can't crack nuts, I don't even like nuts."

"Well someone has eaten them."

"You did."

"Me?"

"Yes. Last time you woke. We had exactly this conversation at the oak tree, where you found your first store missing, and then you came over here and ate up these."

"I don't remember," Redan said. "Squirrels don't remember things very well because they are so athletic."

The robin put his head on one side. "Or stupid," he suggested.

Redan shook his head. "Not stupid. Definitely not stupid. So where shall I go for something to eat? I don't remember any other stores at all."

The robin didn't care. "I eat worms," he said.

Redan looked down his short nose. "That's disgusting," he said. "But this Christmas thing… Are there any nuts involved?"

"Massive nuts," the robin said. "Walnuts, hazelnuts, big Brazil nuts."

"Then it must be for squirrels!" Redan cried. "Who else likes nuts?"

"People do," the robin said quickly. "They'll eat anything. You wouldn't believe what they eat at Christmas time." He glanced around the wood. "Orange balls, and chocolate."

"Do they eat squirrels?" Redan asked the only important question.

The robin shook his head in disbelief. "You really can only think of one thing, can't you? No. They don't eat squirrels."

"I like them," Redan said, looking down through the branches to the man and the little boy and girl. "They don't eat squirrels, they understand about nuts. I like them."

He watched them for a long while. They were going from one tree to another, talking about how tall each tree was, and which one was the prettiest.

"I want one with a squirrel in it," said the little girl.

The man laughed. "All the squirrels are asleep," he said. "They sleep all winter."

The little girl shook her head. "I want one with a squirrel in it," she said again.

After a while the sun started to go down behind the pink clouds and Redan felt cold. He danced down out of the high branch and found a comfortable little corner in a small fir tree. He wedged himself in and curled his tail round. In the morning, he thought, he would make a real effort to remember where his nuts were hidden. In the morning he would find the nut thief and give him a powerful telling-off. In the morning he would explain to the robin that squirrels were indeed the most important animals in the world. In the morning ... or next month ... or next spring ... or whenever he next woke up.

"This one," the boy decided.

"Has it got a squirrel in it?" the little girl asked.

"Oh yes!" said the boy. He winked at his father. "Probably."

The man got ready to dig. "You're sure this is the one you want?" he asked.

The children looked up at the thick dark branches. "Yes," they said. The squirrel, tucked tightly in the trunk of the tree was invisible from the ground.

The spade dug deep into the ground, all around the tree.

"Carefully now," the man said. "We don't want to break any branches."

"Or wake the squirrel," the little girl said.

The man slid the spade under the roots of the tree and carefully lifted it up. The tree rocked.

Redan, cosy and fast asleep, clung a little tighter without waking. He dreamed the tree was rocking in a winter storm. He liked the rocking, he smiled like a baby in a cradle, and stayed asleep.

The man lifted the tree from the hole he had dug. Redan dreamed that the tree was swaying in the wind. The man and the children carried the tree to their car. Redan dreamed that the wind had got stronger and the tree was swooping in a gale. The man lifted the tree on the top of the car and tied it on. The branches closed around Redan in a cosy friendly way, like a pine-scented green cuddle. The man started the car and drove to their home. The wind whistled over the top of the car, hissing through the needles of the fir tree.

"Quite a storm!" remarked Redan in his sleep and gathered his tail around him a little closer.

The car stopped. The man got out and found a pot for the Christmas tree. He lifted the tree into the pot and planted it. The tree quivered as it settled into the pot. "The wind has died down," Redan said in his sleep. "Nice."

The man carried the pot indoors and put it in the window. "Now you can decorate it," he said to the children and went to the kitchen to make himself a cup of tea.

The children twisted the Christmas lights around the tree, and they winked on. "Sunrise already?" Redan enquired sleepily. The lights winked off again. "Sunset?" Redan asked, going back to sleep. The children twisted tinsel around the tree and hung silver, gold, and coloured balls on the tree. They put a little angel on the top of the tree and hung chocolate decorations in the branches.

"Wonderful," their mum said, coming into the sitting-room. "But now it's time for bed."

They argued a bit. "Please can we stay up longer? Please can we do a bit more? Please, you said we could. You *promised*!"

"Fox cubs are noisy tonight," Redan remarked from the middle of the tree where the branches were thick. "Pipe down, please! Someone's trying to hibernate in here!"

The children went up to bed. The mother and the father wrapped presents, and tidied the sitting-room ready for Christmas morning. The house was quiet.

"Thank you," Redan said politely from the heart of the tree and settled himself down for a deep sleep.

*　　*　　*

He woke at dawn. It was warm. It was as warm as a midsummer morning. Redan parted the thick red fur of his tail and peeped out. There was a fire dying in a grate; the embers were still warm. The central heating had come on and the house was heating up, comfortable for people, amazingly hot for squirrels. Redan fanned his tail in front of his little face. "Phew," he said.

He looked out of his tree. The wood, all the other familiar trees, the leaves on the ground and even the sky had vanished. "Golly," said Redan. "Surely the world was there when I fell asleep?"

There was a table below him and on the table was a bowl of peanuts. A little further off there was a fruit bowl filled with apples, pears, bananas, tangerines, and a box of dates. Beyond that was a large bowl of nuts: hazelnuts as big as Redan's feet; walnuts as big as his fists; Brazil nuts as big as his head. Redan remembered. "Aha! Christmas!" he exclaimed. "I knew it was for squirrels, whatever that robin said."

He scampered out of the tree and down to the fruit bowl. He rested on a banana while he tried an apple. The tangerine he spat out: it was too sharp;

but the pear was sweet and juicy. He left wet sticky paw prints as he crossed the table to the bowl of nuts. These were the best. He carried two walnuts back to hide in his tree, but he couldn't resist sitting in the bowl to eat a Brazil nut. He thought it might take him all day. He ate and ate and ate. In the end he just lay back in the bowl and went to sleep.

"Happy Christmas," said Redan.

It was the little girl, creeping downstairs on Christmas morning, who found him. She was expecting to see Father Christmas, or perhaps half a dozen reindeer resting in the sitting-room chairs, so she was not surprised by a very fat, very sleepy squirrel sprawled all over the fruit bowl. She picked him up and tucked him into the green thick branches of the pine tree – she couldn't think where else to put him. And when her mum and dad came down, and wondered at the mess on the table – juice and apple peel and nutshells, and the wrapping off the chocolate tree decorations – she told them that it was a squirrel, a Christmas squirrel who lived in the Christmas tree. They said: "Oh, Victoria, really!"

*   *   *

Redan slept. The cold no longer woke him because it was always warm. Sometimes he stirred a little in his sleep and stretched out a paw without even opening his eyes. Generally there was a chocolate tree decoration within reach, or sometimes the little girl had put an apple in the tree, or a selection of nuts. Redan ate where he lay, in his pine needle bed. He did not care about crumbs in the sheets. He did not care about anything. "Happy Christmas," he murmured and went back to sleep.

Victoria's mum and dad noticed the chocolate tree decorations disappearing, one by one; but they did not mind. "It's the Christmas squirrel," they said to each other, smiling. "Whatever will she say next?"

In January they took the tree out into the garden. Redan, quite a lot fatter, put a hand out and held tight to the trunk. "Storm getting up again," he said, as the tree shook as they planted it in a hole in the garden. It was cold at night, and in the morning it was frosty. Redan, too plump to wake, drew his tail close around him in sleep, and slept on.

*   *   *

"Wake up! Wake up!" the robin said impatiently. "The daffodils are out, the crocuses are out, the snowdrops have been and gone! It's spring!"

Redan rubbed his eyes with his little red paws. "What happened to Christmas?" he asked. He had a faint memory of succulent fruit and rich sticky chocolate and nuts as big as someone's head.

"It's finished. Over and gone for another year!" the robin said impatiently. "Nestbuilding time now."

Redan looked out. The garden was filled with sunshine and there were sweet green buds growing on all the trees. "I'm off to the wood then," he said. "I've got a store of nuts in the oak tree. I remember them well."

"I don't know what you were doing here anyway," the robin said.

Redan looked at the thick green branches which had been his home for the best winter he had ever had. A wisp of tinsel sparkled at him in the sunshine. "That's a rather nice tree, actually," he said. "I shall come again and sleep in it next Christmas."

"But Christmas is nothing to do with squirrels!" the robin said. "I keep telling you. Nothing at all! It's robins who go on all the Christmas cards."

"Yes, but it's the squirrels in the trees who eat the goodies," Redan said firmly. "Ask any boy or girl. They know that every Christmas tree with chocolates will have a squirrel hiding in it somewhere. Who else would eat so many chocolates?"

Billy's Christmas Surprises

Malcolm Yorke

Young Billy Reely-Dulle went downstairs to breakfast one morning in early December. It was always the same breakfast, a bowl of cornflakes, a cup of tea and a slice of toast. As usual his older sister Rosie was seated at the table and so was Mr Reely-Dulle, doing exactly what they did every morning of the year.

Rosie was reading a book while she spooned in her cornflakes, because she never stopped reading books. She read at meals, in her bedroom, in the garden, in front of the TV and in the toilet. This might make her brilliant at school but it also made her pretty boring at home. Billy's father was hidden behind his newspaper reading all the financial stuff and underlining bits with his pen.

"Good morning, everybody," said Billy loudly and cheerfully. His father just rustled his newspaper, and Rosie glanced up from her book and nodded. From the next room Mrs Reely-Dulle called,

"Good morning, dear. Now please don't make any crumbs with that toast." She was polishing the potatoes and putting an extra shine on all the knives, forks and spoons. Already before breakfast she had ironed the newspapers, swept the pavement outside and made a list of twenty-seven jobs she had to do around the house during the day.

Billy sighed and ate his breakfast.

Before he had finished, his gran came downstairs.

"It's a bright frosty morning, Gran," Billy greeted her.

"Humph. Call this frost? When I was young we had *real* frost and when it was bright it was so bright you couldn't see. Not like nowadays…" And she was off. Nothing was ever as good now as it had been in the old days and she told them so all day long. The weather, the food, the manners, and the clothes were all dreadful now compared to when she was young. "And as for that modern music, well, awful, shocking it is! Nothing like those good old tunes we used to dance to when I was a girl I can tell you!" But Billy had stopped listening ages ago.

It was like this every morning – boring, boring,

boring. Billy used to ask his friends round to play sometimes but it was no fun. His sister went to her room to read, his father wrote his reports or added up rows of figures or whatever businessmen did, his gran moaned about today's young people and his mother fussed on about not making a mess or a noise or a spot of dirt. No wonder his friends never came back because, let's face it, he had the dullest family in the whole of this galaxy and probably the next one as well.

Mrs Reely-Dulle collected the dishes and went to wash them twice over and then to launder the breakfast tablecloth as she did every morning. Her husband, dressed in his dark suit, dark tie, white shirt, black shoes and carrying his black umbrella and black briefcase set off to walk to the station to catch the 8.17 to the city. He worked on his financial papers all the way there and back and never spoke to anyone. Billy and Rosie set off for their different schools, Rosie reading as she walked, only looking up when she had to cross the road. Gran settled down to watch the TV all day, tut-tutting out loud about all the awful things people did and said these days, not like when she was young.

Billy soon met up with his friend Jacob who said, "Isn't it great Billy, only two weeks left until Christmas!"

"Yeah, I suppose so," replied Billy with no enthusiasm.

"What's wrong, don't you like Christmas?"

"I like the food and the carol singing and all that stuff, but I hate the presents bit."

"Hate presents! Are you daft! How can you hate presents?"

"Well, like everything our family does they're dead boring. I know now that Mum and Dad will give me new grey trousers, grey socks, grey shirt and a grey jumper. They'll just be one size bigger than last year's and the year's before and the year's before that."

"Is that all you'll get?"

"No, Rosie will give me a book and Gran some spending money and a sermon on how to spend it."

"You're dead right it *does* sound boring. So what'll you give them?"

"Well I'm so fed up I'm really going to give them a shock this year, do something special. So far though, I haven't had any bright ideas."

"What about money?"

"Not as big a problem as usual because I've saved hard all year, and then when my Aunty Mary won on the lottery she slipped me a few pounds."

By this time they had arrived at school and soon they were kicking a ball around the playground before the bell went and lessons began.

Billy thought about Christmas again that evening as he watched Rosie read her book, his father work on his piles of papers, Gran watch TV and his mother vacuum the inside of the kitchen drawers. They were all nice people and he loved them dearly, but they did need a good shake-up.

He went to ask his mother, "Can I go shopping with Jacob and his mum this Saturday?"

"Of course, but remember to polish your shoes first dear, and take a clean handkerchief. Now pass me that doormat so I can give it a thorough scrub."

On Saturday morning Billy took his money along to the shopping centre and he and Jacob went looking for presents while Jacob's mum went round the supermarket.

"Let's start with Rosie," said Billy. "I'm willing to buy her anything except a book, she's already got thousands. The problem is what? If you were her age, Jacob, what would you like somebody to give you?"

"Give me? No problem! A new pair of football boots."

"Right! Great idea and they might just get her away from reading for a bit." So Billy bought a pair her size, black with white flashes down the sides, and luminous yellow laces.

"Now what about my mum? It's got to be something she can't polish or dust."

"Difficult," admitted Jacob. "Does she like music? You can't dust that."

"I don't know – she's always too busy to stop and listen. But it's not a bad idea. What kind of music though? She'll never sit down long enough to listen to a concert."

"Well, a lot of people like dance music, don't they?"

"OK, I'll get some of that. I notice they've got some CDs on special offer in the newsagent's. Now what about my dad? How can we liven him up?"

"That's a tough one," said Jacob, remembering how serious Mr Reely-Dulle always looked with his dark suits and his briefcase full of important papers. "I know, how about a coloured tie?"

"Good thinking, Jake! How about this purple one here with pink elephants all over it?"

"Yeah, that'll liven him up all right!"

So Billy bought it.

"Now we've got the biggest problem of all – Gran. She just watches telly all day and when we're home goes on and on and on about how everything was better years ago. Honestly, Jacob, she drives you round the bend."

"So what you need is something to put in her mouth so she can't talk."

"Hm. Chocolates?"

"No. She'll finish them in a week. You also need to use up all that spare breath she's got."

By now they were standing outside a music shop with a window full of second-hand instruments.

"How about a trombone? No. Bagpipes? No. A trumpet?"

"I can't see your gran with a trumpet somehow, Billy, but what about this saxophone? It's on special offer and you get an instruction book free."

"Terrific!" So Billy bought the saxophone.

When they told Jacob's mum that Billy had bought football boots, dance music, a bright tie and a saxophone, she laughed and laughed. "Well they are in for a surprise at your house. I just hope they like them!" She knew Billy's family and she had her doubts.

At home Billy carefully wrapped the presents in Christmas paper and begged his mum not to look in his wardrobe – she was inclined to polish it inside and out every few days. As Christmas came nearer he began to wonder if he had bought the right presents. Would they really enjoy them?

On Christmas morning the family undid the presents under the tree. Billy was right: he did get new grey trousers, socks, shirt and jacket from his parents, and a book and spending money from Rosie and his gran. They had kept Billy's presents until last and now took turns to open them.

"Football boots!" said Rosie, astonished.

"Dance music!" exclaimed Mrs Reely-Dulle, amazed.

"A funny tie!" said Mr Reely-Dulle, flabbergasted.

Gran undid her parcel and was dumbfounded to find "A saxophone!"

They would never have chosen such weird things for themselves, but because they didn't want to hurt Billy's feelings they all thanked him very politely and tried to look enthusiastic. But privately they wondered whatever they would do with them.

On Boxing Day, Jacob came to call and the two

boys insisted Rosie left her book, put her new boots on and come and kick a ball around with them. She reluctantly agreed. They showed her some tricky moves, how to pass and shoot and head, then they put her in goal and took penalties. Oddly enough she seemed to enjoy diving around in the mud and she brought off some spectacular saves.

"Hey, she's good," said Jacob to Billy when Rosie had gone upstairs to scrape the muck off her knees and elbows and clothes. That afternoon they all three watched the big match on TV together. "Now, this is fun," said Rosie. "Let's get Dad to take us all to the match tomorrow." After a bit of persuasion Mr Reely-Dulle left his business accounts behind and found to his immense surprise that they all four enjoyed the game enormously.

Soon Mr Reely-Dulle had to return to work after the Christmas holidays. He set off wearing his dark suit and white shirt, but just to please Billy he put on his brilliant new purple tie with the pink elephants.

Now usually all the businessmen travelled in absolute silence, each reading his newspaper, but this morning a man sitting opposite Mr Reely-Dulle leaned forward and said, "I see from your tie you're the kind of chap who appreciates a joke. Have you heard the one about..." And then he told Billy's dad a very funny story. The other businessmen listened as well, from behind their newspapers, and when Mr Reely-Dulle guffawed they all joined in and had a good laugh too. Soon they were all swapping jokes and they kept it up all the way to the city. When Mr Reely-Dulle walked into his office that morning even Miss Lemon his secretary smiled when she saw the tie, and so did all his colleagues and he smiled back. It was a good start to the new year and Mr Reely-Dulle thought he might try smiling a bit more often now he'd got the hang of it.

Back home Mrs Reely-Dulle was dusting the ceilings with a long feather duster when she remembered her Christmas present. I'll give it a try, just to please Billy, she thought. She put the CD on and soon her toes began to twitch, then her feet tapped, then she did a twirl with the feather duster. Finally she gave up dusting, kicked off her shoes, and did a wild dance round the furniture. She danced until the music stopped, then played it right through again, and again. By the end of the afternoon she had not got through more than two of the things on her list of twenty-seven household chores. And she didn't care!

Meanwhile Gran had gone off grumbling down to the garden shed. "That's not what I call dance music. Nothing like the proper tunes we had when I used to go to dances." She took her Christmas gift with her and the book of instructions. "I suppose young Billy meant well. It's a silly present but at least saxophones look the same as they did when I was young," she muttered.

First she tried a few tootles and honks and hoots. Then she soon got the hang of it and began to work her way through the instruction book. By the end of the afternoon she had mastered a tune and felt pretty pleased with herself. *I wonder if there's anybody else who'd like to play the real old music,* she thought as she went in for tea. She hadn't been near the TV all day.

Our story now jumps forward nearly a year and by then things were very different at the breakfast table of the Reely-Dulles. For a start they all sat down together and talked about their exciting plans for the day or the weekend. From Monday to Friday Billy's dad now wore a blue or a green suit (and on hot summer days even a cream one) and had a whole collection of fancy ties. The purple one with the pink elephants was still his favourite though. He went off to work whistling and when he got on the 8.17 train all the businessmen there told jokes, played cards or dominoes and did crosswords together all the way into the city and all the way home. He made lots of new friends and he'd been promoted at work. On Saturday mornings he dressed in jeans and an old sweater because he ran a stall in the local market. He sold garden plants with his friend Patrick, the business-man who'd told him that first joke so long ago.

Mrs Reely-Dulle hummed as she glided round the kitchen in her leotard and ankle warmers. After breakfast she would be off to her dance class. When Billy and Rosie were at school she rolled back the carpets and danced and leaped and cavorted and twirled all over the house. She'd bought a lot more tapes and CDs now but the one Billy had given her was still the one she played most.

When Mr Reely-Dulle came home he danced

with her, and on Friday evenings they both went off to the disco – they had even won prizes for their dance routines! The house was pretty untidy these days because she was so busy practising – "But who cares?" said Mrs Reely-Dulle with a laugh.

Gran usually finished her breakfast and hurried off to the garden shed to turn the heating on before the rest of her band arrived. She had recruited a gang of other lively pensioners who played waltzes, quicksteps, tangos and foxtrots and other old-time songs and dances ("They don't write music like that any more," she said). They called themselves The Wrinkly Swingers and played at socials, fêtes, weddings and Bar Mitzvahs. They'd even been on local radio. The drummer, Arthur, used to be a bandsman in the army and he was terrific, a real star. Billy suspected he might fancy Gran because he came round to rehearse in the garden shed more often than the others and took her out for a drink afterwards. "I think we'll make a record soon," Gran told Billy one morning. "Then we can go on Top of the Pops and show you youngsters what good music is really like."

As Billy finished his breakfast this Saturday morning just before Christmas, he could hear lots of Rosie's friends pounding up the stairs to her room. She was the goalkeeper and captain of the local girls' team (they had already beaten several boys' sides and were third in the league). They plotted tactics on the blackboard in her room ready for the afternoon's match. She was still brilliant at school and loved books, but at least now she knew how to have some fun with other people. Most evenings Billy and Jacob gave her penalties practice in the back garden.

Billy sat alone at the table, surrounded by crumbs and dirty dishes. Now his mum didn't bother so much, Billy would have to clear them up himself, but he didn't mind. He could hear disco music from the front room where his mum was jiving, a slow waltz from down the garden shed where Gran was doing a solo on the saxophone, his father laughing and telling jokes while he and his friend Patrick loaded up trays of plants in the garage, and shrill girls' voices arguing about whether or not to use a three-four-three formation came from up above. Soon Jacob and a dozen of Billy's own friends would be round to play and make a lot more noise and mess.

Just sometimes it might be nice to have a bit of

peace and quiet like before, thought Billy. But no, this family could never again be as dull and boring as they were before he gave them their last year's Christmas presents. He smiled when he remembered the changes those odd gifts had caused — it just showed what magic was in the air at Christmas.

He was pretty sure he wouldn't be getting any drab grey clothes this year, because he'd taught the others what fun presents could be. His only problem now was whatever could he give them this Christmas?

The Real Christmas Play

Geraldine Kaye

On Monday most people at Penny Lane School were having dinner in the big hall when Miss Lee clapped her hands.

"Will everybody who wants to be in the Christmas play come back here after playtime, please? All right?"

Mary was sitting at the packed lunch table. But her packed lunch was boring. The sandwiches had too much tomato and not enough cheese and Mum had forgotten her crisps and her banana. Mum had been forgetting things ever since baby Tom arrived and Mary was fed up.

But Mary did want to be in the Christmas play and after playtime she came back to the big hall. So did Sharon and Kylie and Daisy and lots of other children. Mr Bing was busy putting up two big red curtains for the stage. They were the same red as Father Christmas had worn in his grotto last year. This year they couldn't go to the grotto because Mum was too busy with baby Tom.

"Excellent!" Miss Lee said, smiling round at the children in the hall. "In a minute I'll cast everybody, which means I'll tell you what parts you are each going to play. But first put up your hand if you have a real baby doll to lie in the manger and be baby Jesus?"

"Me, me, me," Sharon and Kylie and Daisy called out and three hands waved in the air.

"Excellent. Bring your dolls tomorrow then, you three. It has to be a baby doll with no hair, mind. What about you, Mary, your hand was half up?"

"We've got a real *baby* at my house," Mary said shyly.

"He can't be Jesus, he might cry," Sharon said.

"A real baby is a lovely idea, Mary," Miss Lee said. "But your mum wouldn't let him be in the school play just yet, would she? But perhaps you'd like to be Mary in the play?"

"Yes, please," Mary said.

"Please, Miss." Todd's hand was waving in the air. "If Mary is Mary, Joseph ought to be Joseph."

"Is that all right, Joseph?" Miss Lee said and Joseph nodded. "Boys are to bring woolly lambs or sheep for the stable if they have them but no teddy bears, please. Yes, Todd?"

"Please Miss Lee, what about woolly sheepdogs?"

"No woolly sheepdogs, thank you, Todd. Let's have David for Innkeeper and Jack, Jill and Frances for Shepherds."

"Please, Miss." Jordan's hand was in the air this time. "Jill's a girl and so is Frances. How can you have girls as shepherds?"

"Bo-Peep was a shepherd or rather a shepherdess," Miss Lee said. "Jordan, Leroy and Adil can be the three Kings. Joe can be the moving star for the Shepherds. You hold up a torch, Joe. Annie can be Gabriel, Seth and Beth open and close the curtains and Todd and Ted are inside the donkey."

"Ee-or, ee-or," said Todd and Ted.

"It's a silent donkey, thank you," Miss Lee said. "Christmas plays *always* have a silent donkey. The donkey mask and a grey blanket are in the cupboard and angel wings for two silent angels who stand behind that manger and look at the baby Jesus. Penny and Benny will you be angels, please? And everybody is to sing two verses of *O little town of Bethlehem* when Mary gets to the stable at the end of Scene One and *Away in a Manger* at the end of Scene Two. That's enough for today," Miss Lee said as the buzzer went. "See you all tomorrow afternoon. Don't forget the baby dolls."

"I'm Mary in the Christmas play," Mary said when she got home.

"Oh good," Mum said. Baby Tom was lying in her lap and smiling up at her.

"He never smiles at me," Mary said, dropping her school bag. "I don't think he likes me."

"He smiles at me because he knows me best," Mum said. "Soon he'll smile at you and Dad."

Mary went upstairs and looked at her dolls. She had a baby doll but it was quite old and scratched and her china doll had long brown hair.

"Everybody has a nice baby doll except me. I wish I had a really nice baby doll," Mary said. She was feeling fed up again.

"But you've got a *real* baby brother," Mum said, putting Tom in his little rocking chair.

"Isn't it time he went in his cot?" Mary said.

"Not just yet," Mum said.

On Tuesday afternoon Mr Bing was busy fixing an inn with a wooden door on one side of the stage and Seth and Beth were opening and closing the red curtains. Miss Lee gave out bits of paper to everyone.

"Here are your parts," she said. "But you can use your own words if you like."

Mary read her words out loud. "I am very tired, husband dear. I want to rest."

Miss Lee said, "Boys put your woolly lambs and sheep on the far side where the stable is going to be. Girls, have you brought your baby dolls?"

"Yes," Sharon and Kylie and Daisy said.

"Mary, come and help me choose," Miss Lee said. She looked at the three dolls carefully and so did Mary. Sharon's doll wasn't really a baby doll at all. It had had its hair cut off with scissors and a bonnet put on its head. Kylie's baby doll was very small indeed.

"But she says 'Mama'," Kylie said.

"I'm not sure we need 'Mama'," Miss Lee said. "They're all really nice dolls but I think Daisy's doll is best for baby Jesus."

Daisy was pleased but Sharon and Kylie were cross. "I'm not taking mine home," Sharon whispered and she hid her doll behind the books in the library corner. Kylie put her very small doll in the cupboard.

Mr Bing was fixing footlights along the stage and Mrs Green had come to play the piano and Miss Lee said it was time for a *run through*. Ted and Todd got under the donkey blanket and Mary sat on a stool in front of the red curtains. Then Annie, who was Gabriel, looked over the top and shone her torch and said, "Hail, Mary, you are going to have a baby soon."

"Thanks," Mary said.

"Scene One," Beth and Seth said loudly and they opened the curtains and Mary got on the donkey's back.

Joseph said, "Come, wife, we've got to go off and pay our taxes." He lead the donkey across the stage and back again.

Mary said, "I'm very tired, husband dear. I must rest."

Joseph said, "Here is the inn at Bethlehem," and he knocked on the door.

The Innkeeper opened it. "No room at the inn but there's a stable over there," he said and pointed.

Seth and Beth closed the red curtains and everybody sang *O little town of Bethlehem* and then the buzzer went.

"Very good start, everybody," Miss Lee said. "Tomorrow will you all bring your dressing-gowns, please, and tea-towels for your heads and angels bring thick white nighties. And Mary, have you got a blue dressing-gown?"

"Yes," Mary said. "But it's a bit small."

"Never mind," Miss Lee said. "Blue is best for Mary."

That evening Mary put on her blue dressing-gown and smiled at baby Tom in his cot but he just went to sleep.

"Don't you like me?" Mary whispered.

On Wednesday Mary took her blue dressing-gown to school and after dinner everybody went to the hall. Mr Bing had fixed a manger on the other side of the stage with hay round it and the woolly lambs and sheep. Joseph and the Innkeeper and the Shepherds had dressing-gowns back to front and tea-towels over their heads. The Kings had dressing-gowns too and gold cardboard crowns with fruit gum jewels. Gabriel and the two angels in the stable wore thick white nighties and silvery wings from the cupboard. One of the Shepherds had a woolly lamb under his arm as a gift, the second Shepherd had a feathery white bird and the third a bunch of scarlet cherries.

At first everybody was very excited because dressing-up is very exciting. But once they were dressed ready for the Christmas play something changed. They stopped messing about and went quiet and looked at each other with wide-open eyes. Mary had never noticed before how many sorts of eyes there were, green eyes and blue eyes and bluey-green eyes and brown eyes and all of them were shining.

By Thursday afternoon everything was ready for the dress rehearsal. The hall was full of chairs because the rest of the school was coming to watch.

"Dress rehearsals often go wrong," Mr Bing said cheerily. "So don't let's worry about it."

But nothing did go wrong. Everybody knew their lines and Mary got to the stable at Bethlehem and the Shepherds followed the star (which was really Joe pointing his torch to the ceiling behind the red curtains). But when the Shepherds brought their gifts, Mary noticed that as well as Daisy's best baby doll in the manger like baby Jesus, Kylie's very small doll and Sharon's doll with its hair cut off were both lying in the hay *underneath* the manger. But nobody else noticed because just then the Kings arrived with their golden gifts.

Jordan was first with a gold soap box and Leroy had borrowed his sister's yellow clock and Adil had a brass candlestick. The footlights shone on the Kings' gold crowns and the fruit gums glowed like real rubies and pearls. Mary looked out at the audience in the dark hall. All she could see were eyes shining in the darkness like stars. Afterwards Mrs Green said she had never heard *Away in a Manger* sung so well and she hoped it would be even better on the big day tomorrow.

"Are you coming to the Christmas play?" Mary asked Mum on Thursday evening.

"Wouldn't miss it for the world," Mum said.

"But what about baby Tom?"

"He'll be sleeping in the buggy, good as gold."

"But he might wake up and cry," Mary said thinking of Mrs Green's wanting an *even better Away in a Manger*.

"If he wakes I'll take him out to the passage. OK?"

*   *   *

Then it was Friday afternoon. Everybody was very excited but it was a different kind of excited, a whispery, wondery, fluttery kind of excited.

Mary and Joseph and Gabriel peeped through the red curtains. In the hall people were chatting and waving to each other.

"I can see my mum and my granny," Joseph said. "And four people with camcorders."

"My dad's got a camcorder," Gabriel said. "So has Mr Bing."

Mary saw Mum at the back with baby Tom asleep in his buggy. Mum sat close to the door in case baby Tom woke up and cried.

Mary looked back at the stage then. There were more woolly lambs and sheep in the stable now and a woolly dog too. The Innkeeper was already standing by the door of his inn.

"Are you ready, everybody?" Miss Lee whispered and the main lights in the hall went out and everybody was quiet. The red curtains were still closed and Gabriel was standing on a chair and Mary's heart was thumping. Just for a moment she couldn't think what to say or do.

"Come on, Mary," whispered Seth and Beth.

Mary slipped through the red curtains and sat down on her stool. A bright light came on and Gabriel was there.

"Hail to thee, blessed Mary," Gabriel said. "You are going to have your own baby."

"Oh!" Mary whispered and the light went out and she ran behind the red curtains.

"Scene One," Seth and Beth said and the curtains opened.

Joseph was standing by the grey donkey.

"Come along, wife. We've got to go and pay our taxes," Joseph said.

Mary got on to the donkey's back. She held very tight to the grey rug because Todd and Ted sometimes teased and made the donkey hop and skip about. But that Friday the donkey just walked and its long grey eyes flopped and it seemed to Mary as if she was sitting on a real grey donkey and a real Joseph was leading it along a sandy track to Bethlehem.

Mary said, "I'm very tired, husband dear. I want to rest."

Joseph said, "I will knock on the door of this inn."

Joseph knocked and the Innkeeper came out. He looked pale.

Joseph said, "Can we stay at your inn for the night?"

The Innkeeper blinked and stared out at the dark hall.

"Come along, David," whispered Miss Lee and Joseph knocked on the door again.

"Can we stay at your inn for the night?" he said louder.

But the Innkeeper still didn't speak. The words had flown right out of his head like birds.

"No room at the inn…" Miss Lee whispered.

"No room at the inn…" the audience whispered.

"Bit of stage fright," somebody said.

Mary looked out into the dark hall. Mum wasn't there any more and nor was baby Tom.

Joseph was just going to knock at the inn again but suddenly the Innkeeper said in a shaky voice, "Please come in. Mary can have my bedroom."

"No, no," whispered Miss Lee and the audience together.

"Come along, lad," Mr Bing said and he stepped forward and tripped and the footlights went out.

"Stay where you are, everybody," Miss Lee shouted as Seth and Beth closed the curtains. Somewhere in the darkness Mary heard a baby wail.

"What's up?" whispered Todd as she slid off the donkey and went towards the light in the passage. The buggy was there and baby Tom.

"Don't cry," Mary whispered and he stopped at once. She picked him up and he smiled at her and his eyes were wide and greeny-blue and shining like stars.

A minute later the footlights went on again and the children sang the first verse of O *little town of Bethlehem* and the audience joined in the second verse.

"Scene Two," Beth and Seth said, opening the red curtains. The stable was on the far side of the stage and the donkey and Joseph were there and the two angels with silvery wings. Mary was smiling down at the baby in the manger and the baby smiled back and kicked his legs and the audience gasped.

"It's a baby," somebody whispered. "A real baby."

"How can it be?"

"It's a miracle."

"Look, the Shepherds are coming now, following the star!"

"Hail Mary," the first Shepherd said and he put a woolly lamb in the manger.

"Here's a gift for the baby," the second Shepherd said and he put the white feathery bird in the manger.

"Hail Mary," said the third Shepherd and he put the bunch of cherries into the baby's hand.

"What a little duck!" the audience said and Mary smiled and the baby smiled too and waved his cherries.

Then the three Kings brought their gifts and everybody in the hall sang *Away in a Manger* and Beth and Seth closed the curtains and that was almost the end.

But not quiet because everybody was clapping and clapping. The curtains opened again and the Shepherds and Kings and the Innkeeper, who got a special clap, gathered round Mary and the baby in the manger. Then Mr Bing filmed them with his camcorder and so did the others and a man from the papers took photos and everybody said it was the best Christmas play they had ever seen and however did Mary get a real baby.

Miss Lee said, "Perhaps Mary can tell us?"

"What happened was baby Tom started to cry," Mary's mum said, "so I took him to the passage and he went to sleep again."

"But then he cried again," Mary said. "And I got him and picked him up and he smiled at me."

"Course he did," Miss Lee said. "He's your baby brother."

"Goodbye and Merry Christmas," everybody said. And as they walked away into the cold dark silent night you could still hear their voices.

"Penny Lane School put on the best Christmas play ever."

"A real baby makes a real Christmas play."

"Christmas is a baby."

The Umbrella Tree Fairy

Jean Ure

All year long, the Fairy from the top of the Christmas tree was shut away in a cardboard box, in a small dark cupboard under the stairs. It had frightened her, at the beginning. She had been brought up on a shelf, in a big department store, surrounded by glitter and tinsel and bright lights. The first time she was locked up she thought she must have done something wrong, and that no one loved her any more.

But that had been many long years ago: she was used to it by now. She knew that for eleven months she must stay in her box, but that for just four wonderful weeks of the year she would be set free.

How the Fairy looked forward to those four weeks! The children would come to the cupboard and take the box into the front room. The lid would be opened and loving hands would lift the Fairy out. Her skirt would be smoothed, her hair patted into place, her tinsel crown set straight, her broken wand repaired. Somehow, during those long dark months, her wand always managed to get a bit bent and battered, but the children never minded. She was their Fairy and they loved her!

And then, the big moment ... one of the children would clamber on to a chair and fix her to the topmost branches of the tree, for everyone to admire. There she would stay for four glorious weeks, enjoying the sights and sounds of Christmas, all the fun and the laughter. She did so miss company when she was locked away in her box in the cupboard!

Not that the Fairy was alone in her cardboard box. She shared it with some Christmas bells and Chinese lanterns, with assorted tree decorations and two glass angels, and an Easter bunny who was only let out at Easter. But Christmas bells were silly tinkly things, and the Chinese lanterns couldn't speak English, while the assorted decorations had no conversation at all and the Angels were simply snooty and stuck-up. They were jealous of her, of course, because she went right to the top of the tree whereas they had to make do with the lower branches. One of these days they would probably get broken, and serve them right!

The Fairy's only real friend was the Easter bunny. He was an easygoing sort of chap, though getting on a bit, now. He had been there when the Fairy first came. He knew a trick or two, did the Easter bunny. He was the only one who had the strength to lift the lid of the box, just a tiny chink, so that whenever the door of the cupboard was opened he could peer out and report what was going on. It was always the Easter bunny who told them when Christmas was about to happen.

"They're preparing for the tree," he would say. (He knew when they were preparing for the tree because the children's mother would reach into the cupboard and take out the big red tub that it stood in.) "Any minute now it'll be your turn!"

And then the Christmas bells would start jingling with excitement and the Chinese lanterns would start babbling together in Chinese and the assorted decorations would start jumping up and down and the Angels would snap at them to "Watch what you're doing, can't you!" because the Angels lived in fear of being broken. The Fairy might have felt some sympathy towards them if they hadn't been so horrid to her.

"She's just a bauble ... a mere pagan bauble. *We*

have Religious Significance."

It was because they were jealous: the Fairy knew this. But it was still rather hurtful. Nobody wanted to be a mere pagan bauble!

"Don't you worry your pretty little head about it," said the Easter bunny. "You're still the most beautiful thing in the cupboard!"

So year after year, as the children grew up, the Fairy would be placed at the top of the tree and the Angels would be stuck on the lower branches, and the bells and the lanterns and the assorted decorations would be scattered here and there, and every year was just as wonderful as the year which had gone before.

Until one terrible year when tragedy struck.

"They're preparing for the tree," reported the Easter bunny. "Any minute now it'll be your turn!"

The cardboard box instantly became alive. The bells jingled, the lanterns babbled, the decorations jumped up and down. The Angels snapped "Watch out!" and the Fairy put up a hand and patted at her hair. She hated to be all crumpled and untidy, though the children would soon set her to rights.

And then the door of the cupboard opened and the older child, who was called Tanya, picked up the box. The Angels clung to each other as Tanya ran triumphantly into the front room.

"I've got it, Mum!"

The Fairy's heart began to pound. This was her moment – the moment she had waited for all year long! Tanya ripped the lid off the box. She snatched at the Angels.

"Careful," warned her mum. "They're fragile!"

The Angels looked down at the Fairy and smirked. They had never been picked out first before!

The other child, who was called Kate, pulled at a string of Chinese lanterns. Tanya grabbed a handful of assorted decorations. Kate yanked at the bells. Now there were only the Fairy and the Easter bunny left, and the Easter bunny didn't come out until Easter.

A hand reached in and picked up the Fairy by her hair.

"Ugh! Mum! This old fairy's getting really tatty!"

A shiver of shock ran through the Fairy. One of the Angels sniggered.

"We can't put this on the tree, Mum! Look at it!"

"It's all moth-eaten!"

"It *smells*."

Now the other Angel was sniggering, as well. The Fairy's heart almost stopped beating. What did they mean, tatty? What did they mean, she smelt?

The children's mum picked her up and sniffed at her.

"Mm ... a bit musty."

"It's disgusting! It's coming to pieces!"

It was true that the Fairy's dress was rather torn and ragged. That was because one of the Angels had spitefully poked a finger through it. But it could be mended!

"We need a new one, Mum! Can't we have a new one?"

"They've got some in Allders, Mum. Much nicer than this."

"Oh, all right." The children's mother laughed. "You win! It is Christmas, after all." She looked at the Fairy and shook her head. "I'm afraid this poor creature's had it ... I wouldn't even give her to charity."

With that, she tossed the Fairy into the wastepaper basket. There the Fairy stayed for the rest of the day, stunned by the terrible thing that had happened to her. Helplessly she lay on her back and watched as the Angels and the bells and the Chinese lanterns were hung about the tree. Later on, the children and their mother went into town to buy a new fairy to replace her. While they were gone, the Angels took the opportunity to jeer.

"She's had *her* day."

"Not even good enough for charity!"

"And she *smells*."

The poor Fairy couldn't even seek comfort from the Easter bunny, because he had been taken back to the cupboard.

After a while, she heard the children return.

"This one's ever so much better, Mum!"

"This one's really ace!"

"So she should be," said the children's mother, "the price I had to pay!"

There was the sound of ripping, of paper being scrunched, and then darkness descended on the waste-paper basket. The Fairy found herself covered in bits of cardboard and plastic so that she never saw the new fairy, the ace fairy who took her place at the top of the tree. Perhaps it was just as well. It would only have upset her.

That night, the children's mother took the waste-paper basket and emptied it into the dustbin. It was cold in the dustbin. It was damp, too; and slimy. The Fairy lay shivering, amongst horrible slippy sloppy bits of this and that. Squeezed oranges: old tea bags: cabbage leaves.

Tears rolled down her cheeks. That she should have come to this! She, who had been the pride of her shelf in the department store! She, who had been so loved! How could they do such a thing to her? She couldn't help being old and tatty.

Sometime during the night, the dustbin was raided by a family of foxes in search of food. One of the foxes, who was still quite young, pulled out the Fairy and ran off with her into the street. He played with her for a while, tossing her up and down and chasing her, but then his mother called to him and he ran off, leaving the Fairy behind, in the gutter.

There she lay, unseen, for many hours. It rained, and she got wet. The traffic thundered past and terrified her. A bicycle ran over her wand and crushed it. Her skirt was torn and grimy, her hair was matted, her tinsel crown had disappeared. If the Angels could have seen her, they would have laughed so much they would have splintered themselves.

All hope had gone. It was only a matter of time before she was swept up with the rubbish and thrown on to a Council tip.

And then a boy came walking past, his eyes glued to the gutter. The boy was called Tom and he always walked with his eyes glued to the gutter because you never knew what you might find there.

The other day, for instance, he had found an old umbrella that someone had thrown away. The umbrella was broken, but that didn't bother Tom. He had taken it home and stripped off all the material, until there were only the spokes left, and then he had covered the spokes in cooking foil, so that they were like silver branches, and he had stuck it in an empty paint pot, which he had wrapped in shiny red paper, and hung it all about with bits of tinsel until it looked (almost) like a real Christmas tree.

He had found the paint pot in a rubbish skip and the shiny red paper in a waste bin in the High Street. The cooking foil he had collected, painstakingly, day by day, from outside a local restaurant. The restaurant used it for baking potatoes, so that by the time it reached Tom it was all screwed up and sometimes a bit messy, but Tom just took it home and scrubbed it until in the end it was as good as new.

The tinsel was the only thing he had had to buy. It was amazing what you could find if you looked hard enough.

Last year, when Dad had been with them, there hadn't been any need to go out finding things. But Dad was with someone else, now, and Tom and his mum and Tom's little sister were living in one room in what was called a "bed-and-breakfast" and if Tom hadn't gone out and found things there wouldn't have been any Christmas decorations at all. His little sister, whose name was Joely, thought the umbrella tree was pretty as could be. She didn't mind not having a real one. All that was missing was a fairy to go on the top. There'd been a few tears about the fairy. A Christmas tree wasn't a Christmas tree, wept Joely, without a fairy on the top!

Tom's mum had scolded her and told her not to be so ungrateful – "Just look at that lovely tree Tom's made you!" – but Tom didn't think she was being ungrateful. She was only five years old, after all. At five years old you didn't understand why you couldn't have the things that other children took for granted. Tom understood, because Tom was nearly ten. He didn't like it, but he understood. That was why he walked about with his eyes glued to the gutter. He knew his mum couldn't afford to buy Christmas trees and fairies. It was up to Tom to find them.

And there in the gutter was the very thing he was looking for! Tom squatted down and plucked the Fairy out of her puddle. Oh, what a sorry sight! Wet, limp, bedraggled: chewed by a fox, run over by a bicycle. Old and tatty and long past her sell-by date. But still a fairy!

Clutching her in one hand, Tom ran all the way home. Through the doors of the bed-and-breakfast, up the stairs, along the corridor, into the room that he shared with his mum and Joely.

"What have you got there?" said his mum. (Joely was downstairs playing with her friend Dawn, who lived on the floor below. That was good! Tom wanted this to be a surprise.)

"Got a fairy," said Tom.

His mum pulled a face. "It's filthy," she said.

"Gonna wash it," said Tom.

He tore off the Fairy's ruined skirt, fetched a

bowl of warm water from the bathroom down the corridor and dunked her in it. Oh, how lovely it was to feel all the horrid grime and the smell of cabbage leaves floating away! The Fairy began to feel almost like a fairy again. (She had been starting to feel like a piece of rubbish.)

Next, Tom dried her very carefully on a towel, and fluffed up her poor thin hair with his mum's hairbrush. After that he mended her wand with sticky tape and snipped a length of tinsel off the umbrella tree to make her a crown. Then his mum, very daring, took the scissors to the net curtains (which were all hanging in tatters anyway) and stitched her a brand-new skirt and top.

"There!" she said. "That's better!"

Tom's mum hid the Fairy in a suitcase under her bed, and that night, when Joely was asleep, she took her out and tied her with a strip of tinsel to the top of the umbrella tree. It was a bit of a comedown, being at the top of an umbrella tree in a bed-and-breakfast when you were used to being at the top of a real tree in a proper house, but somehow the Fairy didn't mind. She was warm, she was dry, she was clean, she was safe. At least, she was for the moment. After the dreadful things that had happened to her, she was no longer sure that she could trust what tomorrow might bring. Maybe these children, also, would decide she was too old and tatty and throw her in the dustbin. A tear rolled down the Fairy's cheek. All she wanted was to be loved!

Next morning, the child that was called Joely woke up early, while it was still dark. She switched on the bedside light and looked up at the umbrella tree. Her eyes went round as saucepan lids. She leaned across to her brother and shook him.

"Tom, Tom! Look!"

Tom woke up with a start. "What?"

"There's a fairy! A beautiful fairy on the tree!"

"So there is," said Tom. "Good old Father Christmas! You see? He *does* listen!"

The Fairy was greatly admired. Joely's friend, Dawn, came upstairs to look at her.

"I wish I had a fairy like that," she said.

"You can't have this one," said Joely. "She's mine. But you can share her," she added.

That night, when they went to bed, Joely seemed rather anxious. Looking up at the Fairy, she said, "Will she still be there in the morning?"

"You bet," said Tom.

"Tom, *is* she mine? Is she mine to keep?"

"For just as long as you want her," said Tom.

"I want her for ever," whispered Joely. "For ever and ever!"

And so the Fairy stayed with Joely for ever and ever. She is there with her still – and she doesn't have to live in a box in the dark any more because Joely takes her to bed with her every night.

Just now and again, the Fairy thinks back and remembers her old life, with the glass angels and the jingling bells and the children called Tanya and Kate. She no longer misses any of it, though she does sometimes wonder how the Easter bunny is getting on. Probably, knowing him, he is busy making up to the new fairy. He was always one for a pretty face!

But if ever he grows too old and is thrown out with the rubbish, the Fairy hopes with all her heart that a boy like Tom will find him.

Snowstorm

Adèle Geras

As soon as the tinsel began to appear in the corners of shop windows, and the first red-faced Santas popped up on the television advertisements; the minute the word "Christmas" began to spread itself all over the newspapers, Jake knew. He knew that The Talk was coming. Every year, for as long as he could remember, his mother had given him The Talk. At first, when he was little, he just listened, but for the last few years he had been old enough to ask questions. He didn't particularly like the answers he got, but there was nothing he could do about that. Perhaps one day he'd be really and truly grown-up and not mind at all. It boiled down to one thing in the end: Jake's Christmas was not the same as the Christmas most other people seemed to take for granted.

"Why can I only have two presents?" he used to ask.

"Because I can only afford one," said his mum, "and Santa leaves the other one in your sock." She always added: "I'm sorry." Jake knew that what she was sorry for was the fact that they had no family at all. It was just the two of them, and no one else. Jake's class was full of children who had divorced parents, but this seemed to give them more relations than ever: step-parents, half brothers and sisters, and at Christmas hundreds of step-aunts, uncles, grandmas and grandpas to add to the ones they had already.

One year, Jake said: "It's not fair. Why are we so alone? How come you're a one-parent family, *and* an only child *and* an orphan?"

"I can't help it," said Mum. "And anyway, we've got lots of friends."

"Yes," said Jake, "and they all go back to their families at Christmas." He sniffed and said again: "It's not fair."

"Who said life was fair?" Mum said, and Jake didn't know the answer to that, but he was sure it ought to have been a *bit* fairer than it was.

"We have a good time, don't we?" Mum asked. "We have a tree and lovely food, and snuggle up warm in front of the fire. And I play games with you and we watch all sorts of films on TV. It's fun, isn't it?"

His mum looked so anxious that Jake always nodded and said yes, Christmas with just the two of them was lovely, honestly. Secretly, he waited for the day to be over.

He would have been able to forget all about it for most of the time, except for the fact that everywhere he looked, there it was: in window displays, in classroom pictures, and on all the cards that seemed to be stuck up everywhere. Over the years, Jake had cut the pictures from the front of these cards and stuck them in an album. He thought of it as his Christmas Book, and sometimes he would open it and imagine himself inside one of the scenes. He knew they were make-believe, especially the ones he loved best. For one thing there always seemed to be thick snow on the ground, but where Jake lived snow fell in silly little blobs that melted when they touched the pavement. When they *did* have proper snow, which wasn't very often, then cars and people churned it up into brown slush before you could really enjoy it. There was never, ever, enough to make a big snowman.

Then there were the Christmas trees. Jake and his mum had a tiny little tree made of silver plastic. It lived in a box all year round, and just came out and sat on the sideboard for a couple of weeks in December. There were six tiny, weeny coloured balls to hang on the branches. Proper trees were huge and green and hung with real candles and red satin bows and gold-painted pine cones. Some houses had glorious trees. Jake had seen them, shining in the windows of front rooms, and lighting up the dark outside.

"I know you'd like a real tree," Mum said every year, "but the flat's too small. And our tree is pretty, isn't it?"

"Yes," said Jake, and it was, but it was exactly like the rest of their Christmas. There was nothing actually wrong with it, but it wasn't proper.

Jake sighed. Tomorrow was Christmas Day, and this year was going to be very strange indeed.

"It's going to be different," said Mum, during The Talk. "We're going to have Christmas dinner with lots of people."

Jake held his breath. Who? Which of their friends had invited them? Mum went on: "We're going into the hospital to help give out Christmas dinner on one of the wards, and then we'll have our meal with all the doctors and nurses. Won't that be fun? It'll be just like a party. Someone'll be playing carols on the piano and the ward is decorated ... oh, it'll be marvellous!"

Jake said: "Great!" and tried to sound enthusiastic, because his mum seemed to be so happy about it, but secretly he thought it sounded awful. Who would he talk to? What sorts of things could he do to help? Mum didn't seem to realize that even though it might be Christmas, and it might be a party, there would still be a lot of people around who were ill. They were going to a hospital after all. Jake began to feel a little frightened. What if some people were *really* ill? What if he saw some blood? Or someone being sick?

It was raining on Christmas morning. On the way to the hospital, Jake said to his mum: "Maybe we'll be on a children's ward," and Mum smiled.

"There are no children's wards in this hospital, love. Didn't I tell you? I think we're in a Men's General."

Jake said nothing. It was going to be horrible. To his surprise he found himself longing not for a proper Christmas, but for the kind of day he usually had with his mum, which suddenly, somehow *did* seem like fun after all.

"This way," said Mum and Jake followed her through doors made out of floppy, rubbery stuff that you could almost see through, and on to a corridor that stretched for what looked like miles into the distance.

"We're going to a ward called Elizabeth," said Mum.

"I expect it's down there," said Jake, "where the music is coming from."

They followed the sounds, and sure enough, they were coming from the right ward. Everyone seemed glad to see them. Nurses with paper hats on greeted Jake's mum as if she were an old friend, and a plump Sister with tinsel tied round her hair kissed Jake on both cheeks.

"Welcome," she said. "You're just in time for our carols. Doctor Windshaw has kindly agreed to play the piano for us. And Ladies General have joined us, as it's a party."

Jake looked round. Most of the sick people, men and women, were in dressing-gowns and slippers, and gathered round the piano. Those who weren't well enough to get up were sitting in bed and joining in if they could. Everyone started singing each carol at a different time, and often on different notes, so it wasn't like a real choir, but they all ended up more or less together, and seemed to be enjoying themselves.

Sister came up to Jake and whispered: "Come with me, dear, and I'll give you a tray of mince pies to take round. One of the nurses will follow you with the tea-trolley. We don't want to miss out on elevenses, and the visitors will be here in half an hour."

Giving out mince pies took a long time. Everyone asked Jake how old he was, and what his name was, and some of the old ladies even kissed him and called him an angel, which made him feel silly and also made him blush. He'd only just finished giving out the last mince pie when the visitors began to arrive.

"Come on, Jake," said Mum. "We'll go and sit in the Nurses' Station till visiting is over, and have a couple of pies ourselves."

You could see the whole ward from the Nurses' Station. Jake looked through the glass window. Almost everyone had a visitor. There was wrapping paper all over the floor. Someone's baby had started crying. Sister said: "Some people leave their children in the Day Room watching television.

Why don't you go and have a look and come back later?"

"OK," said Jake. "I know where the Day Room is."

He made his way down the corridor. The Day Room was on the left, but what was this door here? He hadn't noticed it before. He looked inside. The room was completely white. Walls, bedcover, curtains – they were so white that Jake blinked. There was someone in the bed, and he seemed very pale as well. He was also younger than most of the men on Elizabeth Ward.

"Hello," said this person. "Who are you?"

"I'm Jake. I didn't mean to disturb you. I'm sorry. Were you sleeping?"

"No, it's nice to see you. I don't get many visitors. Come in and have a chat. My name is Malachi."

"OK," said Jake. He sat on a white chair next to the bed.

Malachi was very pale indeed. He had hair so fair that it was nearly white, and green eyes like a cat's. He seemed cheerful, but his voice was quite thin and small, and sometimes Jake had to bend closer to the bed to hear what he was saying.

"Do you come hospital visiting every Christmas?"

"No," said Jake. "It's the first time I've done it."

"Tell me about what you usually do on Christmas Day."

Later, thinking about it, Jake didn't know what made him say all the things he said. He told Malachi everything he felt about Christmas, right down to moaning about only having two presents, and never seeing any proper snow.

"I know exactly what you mean," said Malachi. "And I can bump the number of your presents up to three. There's something in my locker that I'd like you to have."

"But you don't even know me," said Jake. "Haven't you got anyone else to give it to?"

"No, I'd like to give it to you. You, after all, have come to visit me. Look in my locker."

Jake opened the locker. That was white as well. It was completely empty, except for something wrapped in gold-coloured foil.

"Give it to me," said Malachi, bringing his arm out from under the covers. Jake looked away quickly. He could have sworn that the young man's arm where it poked out of his pyjama sleeve had something white growing on it. Perhaps that was what was wrong with him. Was it fur? It didn't look like fur. It looked like ... no, it couldn't possibly be

... but what it looked like, in the moment that Jake handed Malachi the parcel, was feathers. He shivered and looked hard at this strange person in the bed. Only his hands were visible now. His sleeves had slipped down and covered his arms, and they seemed normal to Jake. I must have been imagining it, he said to himself.

Malachi spoke: "Open your present," he said. "Go on."

Jake took the parcel and tore off the gold foil.

"It's a snowstorm!" he cried. "That's beautiful. I used to have one when I was little, only it broke." He shook the snowstorm, and white flakes whirled against the glass. "Thank you so much."

"You're welcome," said Malachi. "I hope it makes your Christmas extra special."

"It has already," said Jake, "because it was such a surprise." He looked at the bed. Malachi's eyes were closed, and his face was almost the same colour as the pillow. Jake jumped up from his chair. Getting an extra present had made him forget that Malachi was probably very ill. He must be, to have so little colour in his cheeks, and to be all alone in a room away from the ward.

"I'd better go back now," he said. "I hope you feel

much better soon."

Malachi said: "Oh, I will. I will feel wonderful," but his voice was almost a whisper. He lifted his hand and waved at Jake.

The sun must have come out, Jake thought later, because the whole length of Malachi's arm from the shoulder to the fingertip was edged with fire. Jake closed his eyes to shield them from the dazzle, but when he looked again, both Malachi's arms were under the covers, and everything was white once more.

Jake ran to show the snowstorm to Mum.

"That's lovely!" she said. "Who gave it to you?"

"One of the patients. He's got ever such a funny name. Malachi. He said he had no one else to give it to. I love these snowstorms. Do you remember I used to have one ages ago? That had a snowman in it."

"I remember," said Mum. "What's this one got in it?"

"I forgot to look," said Jake. He shook the snowstorm. "There's a lot of snow, though, isn't there?"

"Yes," said Mum. "Wait for it to settle, and we'll see what's there." She peered into the glass as the flakes cleared. "Gosh," she said. "That's weird, isn't it? There's nothing there at all. Can you see anything?"

"No," said Jake. "Only a layer of white at the bottom here."

"I've never seen an empty snowstorm," said Mum.

"Nor have I," said Jake, "but I don't care. I think it's brilliant. It's the best snowstorm ever." He shook it again. "It really does look like snow, doesn't it, not just bits of white stuff."

"Yes," said Mum. And it did. The flakes drifted down slowly. They seemed tossed by tiny gusts of wind, but how could there be wind in the little glass bubble? Jake stared and stared until the snow was all he could see.

"Put that away now," said Mum. "It's nearly time for Christmas dinner."

"I'm so full," said Jake, "that I can hardly move."

"It was fun, wasn't it?" said Mum.

"Ace," said Jake. "The pudding was delicious."

"Let's go home the long way," said Mum. "Across the park. It'll be nice and empty on Christmas Day. We can go and see how the ducks are."

It had stopped raining, but everything in the park looked grey. Even the grass and the leaves on the evergreen shrubs and trees were dull and colourless.

Jake and his mother stood beside the pond. The water was almost black. The ducks swimming about on it seemed to have no energy. Jake took the snowstorm out of his pocket, and held it up in the air above his head. He shook it, and the small flakes moved in the glass, but not only in the glass. Jake gazed around. The sky, the air, everywhere was suddenly filled with white. Snow was falling, silent and feathery over the whole landscape.

"Look, Mum," Jake said. "It's snowing. Proper snow!"

His mother seemed to have moved away. She was now standing, talking to some people, up on the little hill at the other side of the pond. Where had they all come from? When did she walk over there? And why were they all so funny-looking? Everyone was wearing fur hats, and gloves, and the ladies had long skirts on, and some of them were holding muffs.

"Come on to the ice," said a voice, and there was a boy with ice-skates on his feet standing right beside Jake and holding out his hand.

"I don't know how to skate," said Jake. "And I'm wearing trainers."

"Hold on to me," said the boy. "I'll show you."

Jake put the snowstorm back into his pocket and stretched out his hand.

"I can't believe it," he shouted, as they skimmed over the ice. "I'm skating!"

"Everyone loves it," said his companion. "Look around you."

Jake saw that the ice was crowded with people. They were smiling and waving at him.

"Hello, Jake," said one boy skating past, and Jake answered: "Hello." The truly amazing thing was that although these people were total strangers, Jake felt he knew them all, and they knew him. What was more, they were happy to see him. He belonged to them. It was almost as though they were his family.

Music was playing somewhere, but Jake couldn't see who was playing it. An old man had set up a hot chestnut stall at the edge of the pond, and the coals from his tiny brazier glowed scarlet. The trees, the grass, the top side of every leaf in the park was covered in snow and the black duck-pond had turned into a silver mirror. On the other side of the field, where the park keeper's hut was, the sun was setting. Jake thought it looked like a giant apricot flaming in the white sky, and sending its pale orange rays over the snow.

Jake and the boy spun round and round, until Jake was nearly dizzy. I'm going to fall over, he thought. I must close my eyes or I'll fall over. I'll open them again in a second. He shut his eyes, counted up to four in his head, then opened them again.

"Mum," he said to his mother, "you've come back. Where has it gone?"

"Where has what gone?"

"The snow, the ice, all the skaters…"

"What *are* you talking about?" said Mum. "You must have had too much brandy butter. There isn't any snow, except in your little snowstorm of course."

Jake frowned. Perhaps he'd been dreaming. Perhaps he was suffering from a strange kind of indigestion. He shook up the glass bubble again, and waited for the snow to settle.

"Mum!" he cried. "Look! It isn't empty any more. There's something in it. Can you see what it is?"

Jake's mum stared into the glass and said:

"Oh, Jake, it's so lovely! It's an angel. How come we never saw it before? It's beautiful. Such white wings... When the snow falls, it looks as though the angel is dropping small feathers everywhere. It's fantastic. Who gave it to you, did you say?"

"He was called Malachi. He was in a room all by himself opposite the Day Room."

"That room is called the Side Ward. I didn't know there was anyone in there. Certainly Sister never mentioned it to me, but she was very busy today, wasn't she? What would you feel about going back tomorrow for a while? Sister did say that half the auxiliaries are off and she'd be glad of the help."

"I'd like to go," Jake said. "I can visit Malachi again."

Malachi was no longer in the Side Ward. The little white room was quite empty. Jake decided not to go and ask Sister about him. He felt that that was what Malachi himself would have wanted. Jake took the snowstorm out of his pocket and looked carefully at the angel standing there with snow-flakes covering his feet.

"Thank you, Malachi," he said, with lips very close to the glass. The tiny white wings caught the light coming through the window, and for a split

second it seemed to Jake that fire had touched
them and edged them with bright gold.

The Greatest Gift of All

Jenny Bent

"Tell us a story, Grandma!" begged Emma as she helped her young brother Tim and Grandma shovel snow from the front pathway.

"Well, what type of story do you want?" Grandma asked, pretending she didn't know.

"One about Christmas, of course," giggled Emma, tugging on Grandma's sleeve.

"Well, let's wait until we get back inside the house. It's much too cold out here," she replied. As the words came tumbling out, a long trail of frosty mist carried them away.

Before long, they were all inside the house: Grandma seated in her big comfy chair by the coal fire, with Emma and Tim sitting on the rug beside her sipping hot steamy mugs of cocoa.

"Now, what story about Christmas would you like to hear?" Grandma smiled.

Emma and Tim looked at each other.

"We don't mind," they said.

"As long as it isn't a story about Father Christmas," said Emma.

"Nor reindeer," said Tim.

"Or Christmas trees."

"And definitely not snowmen," they both said together.

"Whyever not?" asked Grandma.

"Because we've heard all those stories a zillion times," moaned Tim.

"You've been very precise about what you don't want. But you haven't had much to say about what you *would* like," she replied.

"Mmmmmm, could it be about lots of Christmas presents?" said Emma.

"Yes, or perhaps even getting one extra special gift," Tim said excitedly. "I like getting presents."

"Who doesn't!" said Grandma. "I believe everyone loves surprises, especially if they come wrapped up neatly in a box. Who would turn down a gift? I can't think of anyone, can you? When you receive a gift it means someone has remembered you. And it's even better to be given something that you really longed for, and not have to hide your disappointment when you get a present you don't even like."

"That's true," said Emma and Tim, thinking back.

"My best Christmas was when Dad gave me a new bike," beamed Tim.

"Well, my best Christmas was two years ago when I got a computer," boasted Emma.

"I know," grumbled Tim. "You never let me use your rotten computer."

"So what! You won't let me near your silly bike!" Emma snapped back.

"Christmas shouldn't be a time to think only of yourselves," Grandma reasoned, "but to think of others too. You should get just as much pleasure from giving as receiving."

She leaned over and picked up a small potted plant from a side table.

"Well, I'll tell you a story from a country far away over the hills and across the sea. This is a simple story about how this little plant we call 'poinsettia' got its special name. It all happened a long time ago on Christmas Eve with the help of a little girl called Maria from Mexico, who surprisingly enough didn't want a special gift for herself, wrapped up neatly in a box. No, in fact what she really longed for was a gift for her family and village. Her family were not very rich, in fact most people who didn't know any better would say they were quite poor. Most of the time they couldn't find two pennies to rub together or even two pesos as they would call it in their own country. You would have thought everyone would be miserable being poor. But you'd be wrong. The Mexican family were good and kind and were rich in many other ways.

"Maria's two sisters, four brothers, mother, father and grandparents always enjoyed good health. The whole family never went hungry. The farm was blessed to provide corn, beans and chilli peppers for them to eat and sell at the local market. Their little wooden house was full of love, laughter and smiles for one another as well as for God.

"Unfortunately, as always in stories like this one, there came a time when hard times, bad luck and sorrow became unwelcome guests in the village. Maria was determined to help her family and people. She was prepared to journey to the other side of the village to get help."

"What was wrong?" asked Tim.

Grandma slowly shook her head before she replied. "Their problem was something we would all find hard to understand. You see, in Mexico cold, frost, wind, snow and rain don't come very often. In fact they never see frost or snow over there. When Maria's brother, José, once told her that snow was like a graceful lady wearing a long white shawl that covered all the house and trees, Maria didn't believe him. But her father, Arturo, told her it was true. So she believed him. But as magnificent and enchanting as snow seemed to Maria, she didn't pray to God for snow. Instead she prayed for rain.

"Her parents, brothers, sisters, grandparents and all the other farmers in the village prayed for rain too. You see, that was the reason why they were sad. You would have thought it was as simple as turning on a tap in the kitchen. But at that time in Mexico if most of the poor farmers wanted water they had to fetch some from the river. And as the sun grew hotter and hotter over many months, the water in the river got lower and lower, until even the fish had to swim further up-river to survive. If no rains came, soon there would be no water at all.

"Therefore they would have no corn, or beans or

peppers, because they would shrivel up and die before they ripened. There would be no crops to sell at the market and no food for the table. If you thought that was bad enough, Maria even overheard her father say to her mother one night, 'If this continues, we will not be able to repay the money we owe the bank. We will lose our farm and be homeless.' That night, for the very first time, Maria heard her father cry.

"The very next day Maria wanted a miracle. Not one that comes in a gigantic mammoth scale, just a small one. She wanted God to open up the heavens to let the rain pour down. So, with her parents' blessing because they felt she was old enough to venture out alone, she set off for the church to ask for her miracle. The bright rays of the sun lit the way to the village church like the star that led the three wise men to baby Jesus in Bethlehem. As she walked the warm dust from the road clung to her bare feet and the gentle winds blew dust in her face. It was Christmas Eve. But, to Maria as she approached the church steps, this day appeared to be like any other.

"The church was a magnificent building, with two tall columns stretching so high it looked as if it pierced heaven itself. Even the tower of Babel couldn't have been higher. The intricate stone carving of Jesus' apostles boasted wealth and splendour. Maria was so overcome by it all she didn't notice a large group of people close behind. As they came up to her they pushed past.

" 'Out of our way little girl.'

"She knew they were all important and wealthy people who had no time to waste talking to poor peasants like herself. But without their help the church wouldn't have been built. She knew it wasn't polite to be ungrateful but Maria could still remember the old church that was torn down. It wasn't grand or large, in fact it was quite small and there was a big hole in the roof. But it seemed much warmer and more welcoming than the new church. Many of her people in her village felt the same and wouldn't come to the church any more.

"Maria peeped around the large wooden doors. Inside she saw most of the richest families of the nearby town whose hearts were as hard and cold as their expensive pearl and diamond necklaces and gold rings. There was Señor Adolfo Pichardo Garcia the town Mayor, Señor Francisco Borge Palacio the town banker and Señor Dante Roma

Ruiz Lopez the town lawyer, to name but a few. These men had done great things, so they said, for their town and nearby village and each of them made sure everyone else knew about it. They were so different from her father Arturo – whenever he helped someone he did so in secrecy. He always told Maria that if you boast about what you do for others you have done it for the wrong reason.

"Each family in the church had a large bouquet of flowers of all colours, shape and fragrance: orchids, flamingo flowers, amaryllis, roses, and carnations. They were to be placed under the statue of Jesus, just like two thousand years ago when three wise men paid homage to the baby Jesus with gifts of gold, frankincense and myrrh.

"Maria was sad. Instead of offering a gift to Jesus she came to ask for a gift for her village. A gift of rain for the peasant farm lands. And as she looked down at her feet she felt ashamed. The dry dust from the roads had made her feet, hands and face dirty, unlike the fine people in the church, who not only wore shoes, but also wore expensive clothes made of embroidered silk and lace.

"Even if I haven't a gift to offer, at least I can wash my feet in the stream nearby, she thought to herself. But what she wanted even more was for the wealthy unwelcoming town folk to have gone by the time she got back, so she could be left to kneel quietly in the church to pray alone.

"Without a second thought she ran down the steps, across the gravel road, and plonked her feet firmly in the middle of the stream. The large smooth stones curved around the contours of her feet. The stream was even more shallow than it usually was. It wasn't deep enough for the village women to wash their clothes in the stream as they would normally do, but at least it was enough to clean Maria's feet. Leaning over towards the cool clear water, she splashed it over her arms, face and legs. It made Maria think back to the Bible stories her father told her, when Jesus was baptized in water.

"Once her feet were as clean as they could ever get, she sprawled herself out on a patch of grass, wriggling her toes in the sun as they dried. She remembered that even someone as important as Jesus had once knelt down to wash each of his disciple's feet. He did this to teach them to be humble. She giggled uncontrollably and thought, It's hard to imagine those rich fine people in the church kneeling down to wash one person's dusty feet, let alone twelve.

"As she looked down the road that led to her home, she knew exactly what her family would be doing at that very moment. Her two elder brothers, Manuel and José, would be helping their father, Arturo, work on the land, digging up weeds from the dry soil with their bare hands. Her mother would be in the house with her youngest brother, Gabriel, making tacos for their midday meal. It would not take her as long to prepare as usual because there was less food in the house to eat. Martha and Romero would be feeding the chickens and milking the cow. Grandma would be busily sewing with Grandpa sitting next to her fast asleep and snoring loudly, while Isabel would be doing Maria's chore – fetching water from the river. The river was now very low and before long would be dried up altogether. Thinking about it reminded Maria she had her own errand to perform, and must return to the church to do it.

"Maria was determined to bring a gift for Jesus like the rich people in the church, but it was impossible for her to buy flowers, as she didn't even have one peso in her pocket. There were only flowering cacti and green plants growing by the roadside and outside the church, but Maria decided that cacti plants would be a better gift than nothing at all. She wrapped her hands in the hem of her skirt to help pick the cacti. Tugging and pulling at the plants, she couldn't even budge them. Maria pricked her finger badly on the prickly needles, and was forced to let go. Her finger bled. But she didn't suffer as much as Jesus must have suffered when he died on a wooden stake wearing a crown of thorns on his head.

"How cruel the people were to treat the Son of God that way, when he had shown others only love and kindness. As she thought this, tears welled up in her eyes.

"She walked slowly back to the church, dragging her feet along the road. She wanted to bring a gift for Jesus but she had nothing. Maria remembered what her mother and father had told her again and again – if she ever had something to say to God she must pray. God listened to a great many prayers and in one way or another in his own good time answered them all. Maria knelt down by the roadside and prayed, a pure and unselfish prayer that would have moved the heart of anyone who could have listened to the words she whispered. As each word was spoken the warm dry wind carried them away. She prayed to God and told him how sad everyone was in her village because there was no rain. She prayed to God and told him all the people in the village were good people, especially her father Arturo. He had such a good heart and had always helped anyone in need in the village or town. She prayed because of her sorrow in not having a gift to bring for the statue of the baby Jesus, like the rich people in the church. All these things she said and prayed for.

"The tall mimosa powder puff tree swayed its branches in pity, while the hummingbird translated Maria's words into song, flying up and up, higher and higher until the melody of song and words reached God himself. It was the best prayer she had ever made.

"At the very moment she finished the prayer, a radiant light, brighter than sunlight, shone directly upon Maria, forcing her to cover her face with both hands. In any other situation, Maria would have felt frightened and run away. But somehow she could sense the light was something good not evil. Standing before her was someone angelic, could it be an angel? Her mother and father had described what an angel might look like. But no one she knew had ever actually seen one. And if they ever had, they hadn't admitted it. But was she seeing one now? His white wings and long white robe was a big hint that he *was* an angel – or a very good likeness of one. Maria wanted to ask him if he was an angel but as she opened her mouth wide, no words came out. She opened and closed it like a fish blowing out bubbles in water.

"'Hello, Maria,' he smiled.

"'H-h-h-hello,' Maria stuttered, not knowing if she should address the person as Señor or Angel.

"'Are you an … angel?' she finally said.

"'Yes, I am. I have been sent to see you.'

"'To see me?'

"'To answer your prayer.'

"'My prayer,' she said, echoing the very same sentences as the angel.

"In a soft voice the angel told her, 'If you want to take a gift for Jesus to the church, pick the wild green plants that grow on the side of the road. When you take the plants to the church put them in the place of honour directly under the statue of Jesus.'

"Maria agreed and began scooping up green plants on the roadside by the handful. The leafy plants grew abundantly just about everywhere so she was spoilt for choice.

"It had no real beauty of its own, in fact it was quite ordinary. It was a plant no one really cared for – it was never picked to be placed in a vase and admired, or even to be eaten. The green plant was treated as a common weed. The leaves were shaped like the green jalapeno chillis her mother used when preparing corn tortillas for the late afternoon meal. Maria knew that when she got home she would help her mother slap small lumps of corn tortilla into thin rounds before baking them on a pottery griddle over a hot fire. The meals at home rarely changed, not even at Christmas.

"Maria was so busy picking a large bundle of plants she didn't notice the clouds slowly gathering across the skies. Finally, when her arms were completely full, she made her way up the stairway leading to the church. All the wealthy parishioners were still there, practically rooted to the spot. It seemed as if none of them had moved an inch. Some of them were even arguing. The men in their suits with gold and silver plated buttons stood proudly, holding their heads up high, while their wives and children shook their heads in displeasure.

"'I deserve to put my flowers in the place of honour underneath Christ's statue,' demanded the town banker, Señor Francisco Borge Palacio. 'If it wasn't for me this fine church would not be built. No man has shown more charity than I.'

"Maria stood silently as she listened to his words. Señor Francisco Borge Palacio owned the bank and the bank would soon take away her father's farm.

"'Don't be absurd. You were not the only one to pay for this church. My family have given money not only for the church but also towards the hospital to help the poor peasants,' bragged Señor Adolfo Pichardo Garcia, the town Mayor. Each family in turn had something to say to support their claim. The fine Señoras and Señoritas shook their fans furiously, snapping them shut in an instant to show their annoyance clearly.

"'My flamingo flowers were brought from Mexico City, from the finest nurseries,' said the town lawyer's wife, Señora Vega de Lopez.

"'So what! My orchids were imported from Jamaica,' snapped Señorita Rosa Chavez Padron.

"'Stuff and nonsense,' said Señora Martha Diaz Lozano. 'My carnations and roses travelled halfway across the world to get here.'

"As Maria listened, she felt any sense of bravery she once had suddenly drain away. How can I place my flowers picked from the roadside in front of anyone else's? she thought.

"So she tiptoed to the far corner of the church and carefully placed the plants against the wall. She knelt down on the cold marble floor to make a quick prayer and creep out as unnoticed as when she had walked in.

"Unfortunately, a small boy with a richly embroidered lace shirt, pointed out Maria to his mother. Before long everyone stopped to stare.

"'Look at those ugly weeds from the roadside she's brought into our beautiful church,' said one.

"'THIS IS AN OUTRAGE!' screamed another.

"'How could this barefooted peasant girl insult our church with such a poor meagre offering?'

"Everyone's entire attention was focused on Maria. They gathered round her. Some laughed out loud, others stood there disgusted by her apparently thoughtless act. Maria was so frightened and embarrassed that her face reddened to a deep crimson red. She quickly gathered up the green plants ready to run.

"But the crowd of people had formed a circle round her, like a roaring beast ready to pounce on its defenceless prey.

"Maria shut her tearful eyes tight and prayed.

"And there, through the stained glass windows, the sunlight flooded through upon little Maria. The light was brighter than any sunlight the town people had ever seen. The church people shielded their eyes with their hands so as not to be blinded. And, suddenly something wondrous happened. The top leaves of the green plant in Maria's hands turned a rich crimson red and the lower leaves turned a magnificent juniper green. Maria stood there clutching the beautiful flowers tied with a bow of silver sunlight.

"And the glory of God filled the church. The people bowed their heads in shame. They stood back as Maria walked up to the front of the church and placed the bunch of flowers under the statue of Jesus in its rightful place of honour. The town folk stood in silence. No man, woman or child dared look up at Maria's face, which glowed radiantly like the face of an angel. The men took off their broad sombrero hats and the women kneeled. As Maria walked away, Señor Francisco Borge Palacio cheered.

"'Our little Maria has been blessed by God.'

"Maria slowly shook her head and replied, 'Señor Francisco Borge Palacio, have you forgotten how my father Arturo walked eight miles to fetch the doctor for your son when he was sick with fever? And you, Señor Adolfo Pichardo Garcia, have you forgotten how my father took care of your prized stallion when it had badly hurt its leg?' Maria's voice became bolder and bolder as she spoke the truth for all to hear, 'And you, Señor Dante Roma Ruiz Lopez, have you forgotten my father was the first man at your side to help you put out the fire when your home was burning down?'

"They all remembered Maria's father had done all these things over the years and much more, helping almost every family present in the church. He had asked for nothing in return for his kindness and they gave him nothing, not an ounce of gratitude or even one peso. They knew Arturo and all the farmers in the village now needed help. Without rain the farmers would have nothing to sell, nothing to eat. They would lose their farms.

The church people bowed their heads in shame to be reminded by such a small girl.

"A warmth began to fill the church which had not been there for a long time. They kneeled on the ground and prayed. Not for themselves. None of them were farmers; they had no need for rainwater; in their magnificent homes, gold plated taps brought water from water pipes far beneath the ground. These people, out of guilt for their own selfishness in the past, now prayed long and hard. They prayed for rain.

"Outside, the wind began to howl, and the white clouds gathered and turned grey, darkening the skies. Finally, small drops of rain tapped against the windows. The rain came down heavier and heavier until it pounded against the church roof. And the whole church rejoiced. 'The farmers' lands will be saved.'

"Maria was taken home triumphantly in a horse and carriage by the rich town people. When they arrived at the village where Maria lived there was a happy sight to see. The whole village was dancing in the rain, Maria's family, José, Manuel, Romero, Gabriel, Isabel, Martha, Grandma, Grandpa, her mother and father amongst them.

Maria got hugs and kisses from all her family and the village and town folk. Maria's father, Arturo, proudly lifted his little daughter on to his shoulders. The rains had saved the future of their farms and everyone was certain to have food for the table and crops to sell at the market. And you wouldn't even guess what happened next. All the wealthy town folk joined in with the dancing and celebrating as well. They all joyfully danced and danced until they were soaked through and even then they danced late into the night.

"From that day onwards the rich town people and poor village farmers became good friends and all helped one another whenever they could. No one ever forgot what happened on Christmas Eve. How a young girl had brought happiness back into her village. If anyone's memory of the day began to fade, whenever they saw the plant Maria had picked at the roadside they remembered. They called it the poinsettia plant: 'flower of the holy night'."

Grandma smiled as she hugged Tim and Emma. It could be said in that little village tucked far away in Mexico, they had truly received "the greatest gift of all".

Sparrow's Special Christmas

Susan Gates

I'm in a really bad mood! Christmas is cancelled. There isn't going to be a Christmas this year.

We're snowed in! When I woke up this morning the whole world was white. We couldn't believe it. Even the weather girl on telly couldn't believe it: "It really took us by surprise," she said.

"I hate you, snow!" I told it. I even shook my fist out of the window at it.

Tomorrow is *supposed* to be Christmas Day. But we haven't got any crackers or Christmas pudding yet. And we haven't got my new bike! Dad was *supposed* to be collecting it from the town today. But now he can't get through to the shops. Not even on the tractor. We've got to wait for the snow ploughs to dig us out.

I asked Mum, "Why do you always have to leave things until the last minute? Why didn't you get my bike before?"

And Mum said, "Because we're so busy. There's so much to do on the farm."

They're always busy. Feeding the sheep, fixing fences, doing all sorts of jobs. They're out there now, seeing if the sheep are all right. They don't have time for Christmas.

And I'm stuck here with Gran. She always comes to our house for Christmas.

"Lucky I got here before the snow," she says. "Or I wouldn't have got here at all."

I just grunt, *"Harumph!"* I'm in such a bad mood. Bet all my friends are having a *proper* Christmas. Bet *their* mums and dads did the shopping on time.

Crash! The front door bursts open. Mum staggers in. She looks like an Arctic explorer, all crusty with snow. Her eyelashes are frozen! They look like they're threaded with little glass beads.

"Burrr," she says, pulling off her boots. "It's dreadful out there!"

"You mean you can't get to the shops?" I ask her.

"We were lucky to get to the top field," she says. "It's really, really bad. Your dad's trying to get the sheep in now."

Gran says, "I haven't seen a Christmas like this since 1947. In 1947 me and your grandad had Fold

House Farm. And we were snowed up there. We had to warm the Christmas lambs up in the bottom of the big oven. It was the only way to keep them alive."

I give a big yawn. I know it's rude but I can't help it. I've heard this story before – about warming the Christmas lambs in the big oven. We don't do that kind of thing nowadays. We've got special incubator things to warm up Christmas lambs. They work with electricity.

Mum says: "It's getting worse out there!"

"Oh no!" I say. "What a horrible, horrible Christmas. Didn't you even get me some sweets – a selection box or something?"

"No," says my mum. "We were going to do most of our Christmas shopping today. We were even going to collect the turkey today. I'm really, really sorry, Sparrow."

My mum and dad always call me Sparrow. It's not my real name of course. Katherine's my real name.

"Look, Sparrow," says Mum, suddenly. "I've got something to show you."

Maybe she did get a present after all!

But it isn't a present. It's a catalogue. Mum

opens it and says, "There's the bike we've got you, Sparrow. I know it's not the same as your real present. But at least you can look at a picture of it."

I'm so mad, I refuse to look at the picture.

"What kind of a Christmas present is that?" I shout at Mum. "A stupid picture? I can't ride around on a picture, can I? I want my proper Christmas present! Not just a stupid picture!"

And do you know what I do next? Throw the catalogue in the waste-paper bin, that's what I do. I know I'm acting like a little kid. But I just can't help it. Christmas should be really nice. Christmas should be just perfect.

"At least you've got a Christmas tree," says Gran. "Look how pretty the lights are."

Then guess what happens? The Christmas tree lights go out.

I can't believe it! One second they're bright and twinkly. The next they're dead.

"Oh, no," sighs Mum. "Not a power cut! The snow must have brought the wires down."

That's all I need. No presents, no sweets, no turkey. And now no Christmas television. This is going to be the worst Christmas ever!

*   *   *

It's Christmas morning. When I wake up the first thing I do is shiver, "*Burrr!*" There's still no electricity. My radiator is freezing cold. When I breathe out, "*Huuuhh!*" my breath makes little white clouds.

There's a bright white light coming through my curtains. I know what that means. It means the snow's still there. Last night I dreamed it had all melted away. And my dad got through to town – five minutes before the bike shop closed. And when I went downstairs on Christmas morning there was a bike-shaped parcel, under the Christmas tree.

Who am I kidding? When I look outside the snow is worse then ever.

"I hate you, snow!" I say, out loud. I make a hideous face at it, through the window.

Might as well stay in bed. There's nothing to get up for. I'm just snuggling back into my duvet when Gran calls from downstairs.

"Katherine, are you awake?"

Gran never calls me Sparrow, she always calls me Katherine.

Her voice sounds a bit worried so I wrap myself in my duvet and get out of bed.

"Ow!" The floor's icy cold.

"Ow!" I've just fallen over my shepherd's crook. It's the one I had for the school Christmas play. Every year I'm a shepherd! Just because I live on a farm. I'm sick of it. Why can't I be an angel for a change? Why can't I have big, silver wings?

I drag myself downstairs in my duvet. Gran's in the kitchen lighting a fire in the old fireplace.

"Pet Sheep hasn't come to the kitchen door," she says.

I haven't told you about Pet Sheep. Sometimes, on the farm, we get a lamb whose mother dies or is too sick to feed it. So we feed the lamb with a bottle. And it gets really tame and it gets used to us. And we call it our Pet Lamb. And when it grows up we call it our Pet Sheep. We've got a Pet Sheep now and she's always hanging round the kitchen door. She lives in the little paddock by the barn. And she comes to the back door for food. She likes Polo mints but don't tell Mum I feed her those. Today, because it's Christmas Day, I was going to give her a whole tube of Polo mints for a present. They're on the mantelpiece, wrapped in silver foil, all ready for her. But she hasn't come to get them.

"Where are Mum and Dad?" I ask Gran. "Have you told them about Pet Sheep?"

"They're digging out sheep in the top field," says Gran. "I hope they're all right. This snow is really bad."

I forget about feeling grumpy. Suddenly, there's a sick, shivery feeling inside my stomach.

"They will be all right, won't they, Gran?" I ask her.

Gran doesn't answer my question. Her face looks grim and serious. She just says, "Katherine, I haven't seen a Christmas as bad as this since 1947."

It doesn't feel like Christmas. Christmas should be warm and bright and sparkly. But our house is cold and gloomy. And I'm worried about Pet Sheep and worried about Mum and Dad, out there in the snowdrifts.

Then I remember something else that makes me even more worried.

"Pet Sheep is going to lamb soon," I tell Gran. "But it's not until next week."

"You sometimes get early lambs," says Gran. "Sometimes they come when you don't expect them."

"Don't say that, Gran. She can't have her lamb now. Not in all this snow!"

The paddock is only across the farmyard. You can see it from the back door. But the farmyard is full of deep, deep snow. It's as high as our kitchen windows.

"We must get to Pet Sheep," I tell Gran desperately. "She might need our help!"

Then Gran starts one of her stories. I can't believe it! This is an emergency! Pet Sheep might be buried under a snowdrift. She might be having an early lamb. All on her own, in this weather. And my Grandma's telling stories about olden times!

"In 1947," says Gran, "in that bad winter, our sheep got buried under snowdrifts. And I was really skinny then, just like I am now. I didn't weigh much at all. Your grandad said I was light as a feather. And do you know, if you don't weigh much you can walk on snowdrifts, you don't sink in."

I was going to yawn. But I stop myself, just in time. And I start listening to Gran's story. I mean, *really* listening.

"I went out to find the sheep," Gran tells me. "I

walked on top of the snowdrifts. I had a long stick and every three steps I poked it into the snow to see if a sheep was buried."

"How did you know when you'd found one?" I ask her.

"They wriggle," says Gran. "When you poke them with a stick, they wriggle, under the snow."

Why didn't I think of that? I'm getting excited now.

"I could walk on the snowdrifts," I tell Gran. "I could do that! I don't weigh much. That's why my dad calls me Sparrow."

"You're not going," says Gran sternly. "If anyone's going, I'm going!"

"I'm coming too. It's my Pet Sheep!"

Gran frowns.

"I'm lighter than you!" I tell her.

"All right," says Gran. "You can come. At least I can keep an eye on you."

I throw off my duvet: "Let's get ready then!"

We get ready in double-quick time. Socks, jumpers, trousers, wellies, gloves, hats. We look like big, fat caterpillars when we've finished.

"And now," says Gran, "we need a long stick."

We look round the kitchen.

"I know!" I tell Gran. "I know what we'll use!"

I clump upstairs in my wellies and grab my shepherd's crook. You know, I'm glad now I wasn't an angel this year. I clump downstairs again.

"Perfect," says Gran when she sees my crook. "That's just what we need."

"Wait," I tell Gran. I clump over to the mantelpiece. Pet Sheep's Christmas present is there – the tube of Polo mints, all wrapped up. I stick it in my coat pocket.

Gran picks up a spade from beside the kitchen door. "We might need this," she says.

We're ready now. Ready to go on a rescue mission to find Pet Sheep!

"I'll test the snow first," says Gran.

And then she does this amazing thing! She opens the kitchen window. She climbs up on to the sofa. And she walks out of the window. She walks right out on to the snow! Just like that!

She bounces up and down on it, as if it's a trampoline! It goes, squeak, squeak, under her wellies. But she doesn't sink in.

"It's nice and firm," says Gran. "You can come out now."

So I climb out of the window too.

And we're walking on top of snowdrifts, me and Gran! The snow's crunchy and creaky but we don't sink. The sun comes out and makes the snow bright and sparkly. And it's really Christmassy. It's brilliant. It's like walking on top of a giant Christmas cake!

But then I start worrying about Pet Sheep.

I'm getting cold now. *Clack, clack, clack*. What's that noise? It's my teeth.

"Here's the paddock, Gran!"

We nearly missed it. Because all you can see is the top of the paddock wall, poking above the snow.

"Start sliding the crook in," says Gran. "Gently, gently," she warns. "And try close to the wall. That's where sheep like to shelter."

I slide in my shepherd's crook. Did something wriggle? Or is it me shivering?

"No," says Gran. She's listening hard. Listening for scuffling sounds deep under the snow. "Nothing there. Try this place here."

We try and try. We scrunch round the paddock. And every three steps we poke another hole. But we don't find anything. Nothing wriggles under the snow.

I'm so cold and tired I'm nearly crying. The sun has gone in. "More snow on the way," says Gran, looking at the grey clouds.

"We'll never find Pet Sheep!" I say.

And I nearly give up. But my little gran doesn't give up. She doesn't seem to feel the cold. She's tough, my gran. She can chuck hay bales about. I've seen her. Not many grans can do that.

"Let's try over there," she says.

I trudge after her. I've got three pairs of socks on but my toes are like ice-pops. I've got gloves on but my fingers are stinging like mad and I want to go back and...

Whoops! I've tripped over something. I crash to my knees and my hand reaches out and grabs something: "Urgh, what's that?" It's wool, all crispy with ice.

"Pet Sheep!" I cry. "It's Pet Sheep!"

Pet Sheep isn't buried very deep. I start digging like mad with my hands like a dog digging up a bone. There's snow flying all around. But Gran gently pushes me out the way. I forgot she'd brought a spade.

Very carefully, she starts to dig. And soon I see Pet Sheep's head.

"She's all right. Look, she's all right."

"Baaa!" says Pet Sheep.

"Come with us, girl," I tell Pet Sheep. "You're only a little sheep. You can walk on the snow too."

But Pet Sheep doesn't move. She doesn't wriggle free. She just stays in her hole in the snow.

I unwrap her Christmas present. "Come on girl, come on!" I hold out a Polo. But even a Polo mint won't make her follow me.

"I think I know what's wrong," says Gran.

Gently, very gently, she clears more snow away. She does it with her hands, not the spade. And she finds a soggy little bundle.

I peer into the hole in the snow: "It's a lamb!"

"She won't come without her lamb," says Gran.

Gran lifts out the lamb and it's floppy. It's legs are all dangly.

"Is it dead?" I ask her.

"Nearly," says Gran. "We'd better hurry back."

As fast as we can, we start plodding back to the house. I carry the crook and the spade. Gran hugs the lamb to her coat. Pet Sheep scrambles out of the hole and comes trotting after us.

It's starting to snow again. Big soft flakes that stick to your face.

"Hurry!" says Gran, urgently.

I can't see where we're going. The world is all white and whirling. But Gran knows the way. And soon we're crawling back through the kitchen window.

"What about Pet Sheep?"

Pet Sheep pokes her head through the window: "Baaaa!"

"Leave her outside," says Gran. "We'll see to her in a minute. It's her lamb I'm worried about."

The lamb's eyes are closed.

"We'll have to warm it up," says Gran.

"I'll get the incubator!" I go racing off. I know where it is. It's in the storeroom, under the stairs.

Then I remember, "Oh no!"

There's no electricity.

Gran takes the lamb close to the fire. But it still looks dead. "Poor little mite," says Gran.

I nearly ask: "What did you do in 1947, Gran?" But then I remember. They warmed lambs up in the bottom of the big oven. And guess what? Our oven's electric.

But my gran isn't beaten yet.

"Have you got any baking foil?" she asks me. "You know, the silver kind, that comes on a roll?"

"Yes, we have!"

I know we have because my mum's got some extra-wide foil for the Christmas turkey. But we couldn't collect the turkey so we don't need it any more, do we?

I grab the foil from a cupboard and Gran tears off a big piece. Then she wraps the lamb in it!

"That'll keep it warm," she says.

My gran's a genius. She really is.

"Have you got a cardboard box?"

"There's the box that we keep the Christmas tree decorations in."

"That'll do."

So we put the lamb in the box. It looks like a Christmas present, all done up in silver wrapping. We put the box by the fire. Then we sit and wait.

"Baa!" goes Pet Sheep outside the window. She's worried about her baby.

"It's all right, Pet Sheep!" I call out to her in a cheerful voice. "You can have your baby back in a minute. But we've got to warm it up first!"

But I don't feel cheerful. The lamb isn't moving at all.

"Please let it be alive!" I wish. "Please let it be alive. It'd be the best Christmas present ever!"

But the lamb still doesn't move.

Gran shakes her head. "It's been out in the cold too long," she says, sadly.

I feel really sad too. As if there's a heavy stone inside me. I get up from the fire. I drag myself over to the window one … step … at … a … time. I don't want to do it. But I've got to. I've got to tell Pet Sheep what's happened.

"Hang on a minute," says Gran.

She peers into the box. I rush back and peer into the box too.

The silver foil's going all crinkly, as if there's something twitching inside it.

"Maaa!" says the lamb, in a tiny voice. "Maaa!"

The front door crashes open. A gust of snow blows in. And there are Mum and Dad. They've come back safe from the snowdrifts! They're stomping around to keep warm. Slapping the snow off their clothes.

"Are you all right, Sparrow?" asks Dad.

"Dad! We've rescued Pet Sheep. Me and Gran did it. We walked on the snowdrifts. We dug her out. She's got a lamb! And look, it's still alive!"

I'm in bed, wrapped in my duvet. I'm warm

because I've got two hot-water bottles. Christmas Day is nearly over.

What a funny Christmas Day! It wasn't a proper Christmas. We didn't have crackers or turkey or a selection box. We ate soup warmed up on the fire. Then we warmed up tinned rice pudding for afters.

But Pet Sheep's lamb grew stronger and stronger. She was going, "MAAA! MAAA!" while we ate our Christmas dinner. She was standing up on wobbly legs. As soon as we knew she was all right we gave her back to Pet Sheep. They're out in the barn, with lots of hay to keep them warm. So I've got a Pet Sheep and Pet Lamb now. Wonder if Pet Lamb likes Polos as much as her mum?

You know that catalogue that I threw away? With the picture of my Christmas bike in it? Well, I went to get it out of the waste-paper bin. It was all crumpled up so I smoothed it out. And do you know what? It's a beautiful silver bike. I can't wait to get it. I've cut the picture out and put it under my pillow. But I keep taking it out and putting my torch on so I can have another look.

It wasn't a *proper* Christmas. But it was a special Christmas. I'll never forget it. And when I get really old, like Gran, I'll tell everyone about it.

About the special Christmas when we had soup for our Christmas dinner. When Gran and me walked on snowdrifts and dug out Pet Sheep. And saved Pet Lamb's life by wrapping her in silver foil that was meant for the Christmas turkey!

Dear Santa

Tessa Krailing

T homas was halfway through a slice of pizza when Dad dropped his bombshell. "By the way, kids," he said casually, "we shan't be spending Christmas at home this year. We're going up north to spend it with Grandad."

Thomas stopped eating and stared at him with his mouth open.

"Oh, brilliant!" said Kerry, his older sister. "Will there be snow?"

"Almost certainly," said Mum. "Thomas, please close your mouth. A half-chewed piece of pizza is not a pretty sight."

Thomas finished chewing and swallowed hastily. "But – but we can't," he stammered. "We can't go away at Christmas."

"Why not?" asked Dad.

Thomas went red. "Because – because we never go away at Christmas. We always spend it at home."

"Oh, don't be such a stick-in-the-mud," said

Kerry. "It'll be fun at Grandad's. You were only a baby last time we visited him so you don't remember what it's like. We'll be able to build a snowman and go sledging and all that sort of stuff."

"Besides," said Mum, "the poor old man will be on his own this year, so it's only right we should go and keep him company. Nobody should be left alone at Christmas."

"But why can't he come down south to us?" asked Thomas.

"Because he has to stay and look after the animals," said Dad. "It gets very cold up north in December. He can't possibly leave the herd at this time of year."

Thomas pushed his plate away. Suddenly he couldn't eat any more.

Mum gave him a curious look. "What's the problem, Thomas? Why don't you want to spend Christmas with Grandad?"

"I'd rather stay at home," Thomas mumbled.

"Well, you can if you like," said Dad. "But it'll be pretty miserable here on your own. No Christmas dinner…"

"No tree," said Mum.

"And no presents!" said Kerry with a grin.

Thomas went even redder. He pushed back his chair and ran upstairs to his room and threw himself on the bed.

What on earth was he going to do?

A week ago he had sent a letter to Santa asking for certain things he would like for Christmas. Well, one certain thing in particular – a pair of rollerblades. His eyes misted over, just thinking about them. He didn't care about anything else. He wouldn't even mind if he had only one present this Christmas, as long as it was a pair of roller-blades. He'd shown Mum the letter before he sent it and she said she thought there was a fair chance he might be lucky.

But if they went to stay with Grandad for Christmas, *how would Santa know where to deliver their presents?*

No one else seemed troubled about it. They obviously hadn't realized this could be a major problem. It wasn't that he didn't want to stay with Grandad. He loved Grandad. At any other time of year he would be only too happy to go up north and keep him company.

But he didn't want to be away from home at Christmas.

Thomas knelt on the bed to study the racing car calendar over his bed. Today was 10 December. What if he wrote another letter, telling Santa about the change of plan? Would it reach him in time?

He took out his writing pad and wrote a note in his best and clearest handwriting:

DEAR SANTA,
WE SHAN'T BE HOME THIS CHRISTMAS.
WE ARE GOING UP NORTH TO STAY WITH
GRANDAD.
LOVE, THOMAS
PS: IT WAS ROLLERBLADES.

Just as he finished the envelope there came a knock at the door. Hastily he folded the piece of paper and stuffed it inside.

Mum's head appeared round the door. "It's only me," she said. "Thomas, are you feeling all right?"

"Yeah, fine," he assured her. And it was true, he felt a lot better now.

"Only you seemed a bit upset downstairs. You don't really mind going to stay with Grandad, do you?"

"No, I don't mind." He covered the envelope with his hand.

"What have you got there?" Mum asked.

"Er – just a letter."

"You've written a letter?" She looked astonished. "Who to?"

"Um, well, er—" He decided to tell the truth. "I thought I'd better let Santa know we'll be at Grandad's for Christmas. Otherwise ... well, he might deliver our presents to the wrong address."

"Oh, I see. How sensible of you." She gave him a teasing look. "Is that why you didn't want to go away?"

"Well ... yes, I suppose it was."

"Oh, Thomas! Why didn't you say so?"

"I was afraid you'd think I was stupid."

"Of course I wouldn't. Here, give me the letter." She held out her hand. "I'll post it for you."

"Thanks." He gave it to her.

No sooner had she left the room than Thomas remembered it had no stamp. Would she notice? He'd better make sure. He ran down the stairs after her, but when he reached the door of the living-room he heard voices and stopped.

"...written this letter," Mum was saying. "He was afraid that Santa wouldn't know where he'd gone."

Dad chuckled softly. "Poor Thomas. Do you

think we should tell him yet?"

"No, he's still very young. Let's leave it a while longer."

Thomas felt deeply hurt. Mum had promised she wouldn't think he was being stupid and now she was laughing about him with Dad. And what was it they didn't think they should tell him yet? He hated secrets – unless of course he was the person keeping them. Did Kerry know? His whole family seemed to be ganging up on him.

Fed up, he turned round and stomped back upstairs. Some rotten Christmas this was going to be, stuck in the frozen North with no presents!

On Christmas Eve they packed everything into the car and set off for Grandad's. The journey on the motorway took hours. Hours and hours and hours. And all the while it was getting colder. Colder and colder and colder. When they got out of the car at a service station their breath froze on the air. "Anyone fancy some hot soup?" asked Mum taking out a Thermos.

"OK, but we mustn't stop long," said Dad. "We've still a long way to go."

They drank chicken soup out of mugs and set off

again. This time Mum did the driving. She and Dad had agreed to take it in turns because it was such a long journey.

Soon Thomas fell asleep, resting his head against Kerry's shoulder. In his dreams he saw his home, dark and shuttered and empty, and Santa peering down the chimney.

"Well, here's a rum thing," Santa muttered under his breath. "No one at home. I'll have to give their presents to someone else. Ah well, I daresay some young boy or girl will be delighted to receive these rollerblades…"

Thomas awoke with a start. "No!" he shouted. "No, don't do that!"

"Don't do what?" asked Kerry. "I haven't moved for the last half hour. Could you sit up, please? I've got cramp in my arm."

Then he realized that he was still in the car. Still travelling north. Still on the way to Grandad's.

And it was still Christmas Eve.

He peered out of the window and saw they were no longer on the motorway but travelling along a straight, narrow road lined with fir trees. "Where are we?" he asked. "Are we nearly there?"

"Not yet," said Dad from the driving seat. He

and Mum must have changed over while Thomas was asleep.

On and on they sped. Soon the countryside began to look different, more rugged and hilly, with fast moving rivers. Thomas began to feel drowsy again. He drifted in and out of sleep, only half aware of arriving at a port … and driving on to a ferry … and driving off again. Next time he woke up properly they were crossing a narrow bridge over a ravine.

"Oh, good," said Kerry. "It's starting to snow."

Large white flakes fluttered down from the sky and burst against the windscreen. Before long, Dad had to switch the wipers on. Soon he could hardly see where he was going. He slowed his speed right down, peering through a lacy curtain of ice at the fast-disappearing track.

"I hope we make it before dark," Mum said anxiously. "It would be awful if we had to spend Christmas huddled inside the car."

"Oh, we'll make it," said Dad, trying to sound confident. "It's not much further. It can't be."

"I'm hungry," complained Kerry.

Thomas didn't say anything. Miserably he stared through the car window at the wintry scene outside, wishing he was at home by the fire.

Then, just when he had given up hope of ever arriving anywhere, Dad said, "There it is! Look, on our left. I can see a light in the window."

"Oh, thank goodness!" Mum sounded ready to cry with relief.

At that moment the car skidded sideways and came to a stop. Dad tried to get it started again, but it refused to budge. He got out to investigate.

"We've run into a snowdrift," he reported. "You'd better get out. We'll have to walk the last bit."

It was freezing outside. Through deep snow they made their way towards Grandad's house, past the barn where the animals were kept, past the garage and the outhouses. By the time they reached the front door Thomas's jeans were soaked, his feet felt like blocks of ice and his hands were numb.

Then, suddenly, the door opened and Grandad stood there, beaming all over his red, cheerful face.

"At last!" he exclaimed. "I was beginning to worry about you. Come in, come in!"

They trooped inside. Grandad hugged them one by one, scratching their cheeks with his bushy white beard.

"My, how you've grown!" he remarked when it was Thomas's turn. "Yet it can't be more than a year since I came down south to visit you."

"Eighteen months," said Mum, taking off her coat. "And far too long since we last came north. I must say you've made it look very cosy and welcoming."

Grandad beamed at her. "I'm glad you think so."

The house was old, with thick stone walls and dark beams, but Grandad had strung up tinselly decorations and coloured lights. Festoons of cards hung from the rafters and in one corner stood a huge Christmas tree, reaching almost to the ceiling. Thomas began to feel more cheerful.

Until Dad remarked, "I see you've made some alterations. That gas fire's new, isn't it."

Grandad nodded. "New this year. So much more convenient than having to fetch coal in from outside."

Oh, no! Thomas stared in horror at the large, modern gas fire with its pretend flames flickering around pretend coals. It completely filled the fireplace, leaving no gaps anywhere.

How on earth could Santa deliver their presents if the chimney was blocked up?

He couldn't think of anything else all evening. During supper he kept imagining Santa trying to get through and finding himself stuck behind the gas fire. What would he do? Would he give up in disgust – or, worse, would he be trapped there for ever and ever?

"This stew is wonderful, Grandad," said Kerry. "It's warming me right through."

"That's good," he said. "Thomas, you're very quiet. Don't you like it?"

Startled, Thomas looked up. "Like what?"

"The stew, dimwit!" said Kerry.

"He's tired out after the journey," Mum said quickly. "I think he should go to bed pretty soon."

For once Thomas didn't argue.

"I've put you in the attic," Grandad explained as he took him upstairs. "The bed's a bit narrow but it should be comfortable as long as you don't try to move about too much." He opened the door and switched on the light. "There. Think you can manage?"

"Yes, thanks," said Thomas.

Grandad smiled at him kindly. "It's very good of you to come all this way to see me. I expect you'd far rather have stayed at home for Christmas."

Thomas was tempted to tell the truth, but he didn't want to hurt Grandad's feelings. "No, it's OK," he said gruffly. "I expect I'll enjoy it when I'm not so tired."

"Good boy." Grandad patted his shoulder. "Give me a yell if you need anything." He closed the door and left.

When Thomas had washed and undressed he went to look out of the window. At last it had stopped snowing. A brilliant moon lit up the scene, casting blue shadows over the frozen countryside. Below him lay a large white square of snow with not a mark on it, not even a footprint. It looked like a blank sheet of paper...

Suddenly he had a brilliant idea!

He pulled on his dressing-gown and crept downstairs, past the living-room where everyone was talking and laughing, until he came to the boots he was wearing when he arrived. He pulled them on, quietly opened the front door and stepped outside.

It didn't seem so cold now that it had stopped snowing. Everywhere was silent, except for slight sounds of movement in the barn where the animals were kept. His boots made a scrunching noise in the snow, leaving a deep imprint. As soon as he reached the large white square he began to tread with care, turning and twisting as he spelt out the message with his footprints:

DEAR SANTA
    DON'T TRY TO COME DOWN THE CHIMNEY
    LOVE, THOMAS

When he had finished he stood still and read over what he had written. To be honest, it looked a bit of a mess from down here, just a lot of downtrodden snow, but from above the message should be easy to read. At least it would save poor Santa getting stuck behind the gas fire – and with luck he might find somewhere else to leave their presents.

Thomas walked back to the front door. He opened it quietly and stepped into the hall. As he took off his boots he heard the others still talking in the living-room.

"...so he actually wrote a letter to Santa!" That was Dad's voice, shaking with laughter.

"And I offered to post it for him!" said Mum.

Thomas went hot all over. So they still thought he was a big joke, just because he'd tried to let Santa know where he'd be spending Christmas. Well, if they looked outside the front door they'd probably laugh even louder.

Then Kerry said, "I think we should tell him. Don't you, Grandad?"

"No need," said Grandad. "He'll find out for himself when the time is right."

Now they were talking about the secret again. It must be something they all knew about, even Grandad. This time Thomas felt more angry than hurt. He was on the point of bursting into the room and demanding to know what it was when he heard Grandad say, "Well, it's time I went and did my duty. The animals will be getting restless."

"You'd better wrap up well," said Mum. "It's very cold out there."

"Don't worry, my old fleecy coat keeps me warm as toast."

The living-room door started to open. Guiltily Thomas shot up the stairs just as Grandad came out into the hall. He went back into the attic bedroom and looked out of the window.

Oh, no! Even seen from above, the words were

very difficult to read. His footprints seemed to wander all over the place and the letters weren't at all clear. It was hard to tell the 'D's from the 'O's, the 'M's looked more like 'W's and the 'E's and 'S's like figure 8's. In fact the message appeared to say:

O8AR 8ANTA
   OONT TRY TD CDW8 OOWN TH8 CHIWN8Y
   LDV8, THDWA8

And then there was a long, wavering line where he had made his way back to the front door. Thomas groaned. Santa would *never* be able to read it, not even if he was looking down at it from above.

At that moment the front door opened and Grandad appeared below, dressed in a bulky coat with a hood. He set off towards the barn without even glancing at the churned-up snow in front of the house.

The animals seemed to hear him coming. They stamped their feet as he approached and Thomas heard a faint jingling sound, as if they were wearing some kind of harness. Grandad opened the barn door and went inside.

A few minutes later he reappeared, leading a line of deer. At least, Thomas supposed they must be deer because they had antlers. In fact they looked more like – yes, how strange, they looked more like reindeer. But of course that was impossible. If Grandad kept reindeer surely someone would have mentioned it? But they hadn't. They'd only ever said he kept animals and couldn't leave the herd at this time of year. They'd never said anything about *reindeer*!

Thomas pressed his face to the window. He watched as Grandad sorted the animals into pairs and hitched them to an enormous sledge he brought out of the garage. Then he climbed on to the sledge and shook the reins. The reindeer started forward, straining at the harness. Slowly, gradually the sledge began to move, gathering speed as it slid over the snow. As it passed his window Thomas just had time to see that it was laden with presents…

So *that* was the secret!

No wonder the others hadn't worried about coming north for Christmas!

No wonder they'd all thought it so funny when he wanted to let Santa know his change of address!

Because there was no need. Santa knew exactly where he was spending Christmas.

Because Santa was Grandad!

The sledge took off into the sky. Thomas stared upwards, watching as it circled the house. Was Grandad trying to read the message in the snow? Well, it didn't matter if he couldn't. It didn't matter one little bit. A broad grin spread over Thomas's face. Even the rollerblades didn't seem important any more. No presents on earth could compare with the wonderful discovery he'd made tonight.

He'll find out when the time is right, Grandad had said.

Well, now he *had* found out. And the time was exactly right.

Yawning, Thomas climbed into the narrow bed. Suddenly he felt very, very tired. In no time at all he fell asleep.

MAGICAL CHRISTMAS STORIES

With stories by Malorie Blackman,
Gillian Cross and Jean Ure

If you adored *Wondrous Christmas Stories*,
you'll love reading *Magical Christmas
Stories*, too. With eleven seasonal tales
by best-selling authors, this collection
will bring a glow to even the coldest
winter's day.

Open it up and discover how magical
this day truly is.